About the Author

While I was growing up, my father was in the RAF. This meant that every two years our family would pack up and move to another RAF base. As you can imagine I had plenty of schools and dozens of friends – most of whom I got to know only briefly.

One of the things that stood still during my childhood were the stories I used to fetch from the local library. Even if we'd ended up in some remote desert air force station, I always knew that a book could take me into a world filled with people trying to sort out problems often ten times more interesting than my own.

I've written stories and poems since then. Sometimes based on things that have happened to me, sometimes on topics that I'm just interested in. The ideas grow from small incidents – people moving house, starting a new school – which can be transformed into something exciting by simply applying the magic question:

'What if—?'

Nick Manns

Also published by Hodder Children's Books

Skellig
Kit's Wilderness
Heaven Eyes
Counting Stars
David Almond

Blackthorn, Whitethorn
THE MOVING TIMES TRILOGY
Bloom of Youth
Grandmother's Footsteps
Stronger than Mountains
Rachel Anderson

A Secret Place
The File on Fraulein Berg
Odd Girl Out
Joan Lingard

The Fated Sky
Chance of Safety
Henrietta Branford

Hauntings
Nightcomers
The Story Collector
Telling Tales
Susan Price

The Apostle Bird
The Divine Wind
Garry Disher

Secret Songs
Jane Stemp

Control-Shift

Nick Manns

a division of Hodder Headline Limited

For Bel
who didn't give up

First published in Great Britain in 2000
by Hodder Children's Books

10 9 8 7 6 5 4 3

A Catalogue record for this book is available from the
British Library

ISBN 0 340 76511 9

Typeset by Avon Dataset Ltd, Bidford-on-Avon, Warks
Printed and bound in Great Britain by
The Guernsey Press Co. Ltd, Channel Isles

Hodder Children's Books
a division of Hodder Headline Limited
338 Euston Road
London NW1 3BH

What we are today comes from our thoughts of yesterday, and our present thoughts build our life of tomorrow: our life is the creation of our mind.

If a man speaks or acts with an impure mind, suffering follows him as the wheel of the cart follows the beast that draws the cart.

The Dhammapada

What we are today comes from our thoughts of yesterday, and our present thoughts build our life of tomorrow: our life is the creation of our mind.

If a man speaks or acts with an impure mind, suffering follows him as the wheel of the cart follows the beast that draws the cart.

The Dhammapada

Preface

by Dr Theresa Davies, Clinical Psychologist at St Margaret's Hospital, Craybourne

There comes a time in every physician's career when she or he is confronted by a case that is so baffling, so much at odds with notions of common sense that they are forced to concede that science doesn't hold the answer to all the great mysteries. Well at least not yet.

It is barely two years since the Hayton case made the headlines; barely two years since the trial brought forth some of the most sensational evidence ever to grace the stage of an English law court.

Inevitably, because of the nature of that evidence, many people regarded the testimony as being the work of an overexcited imagination – and an immature imagination at that.

In the weeks that followed, who can forget the thousands of column inches that were devoted to explaining – or decrying – the paranormal? Indeed, who can forget the number of celebrities who claimed to be in touch with figures from the distant past?

However, although the prosecution was to ridicule the sworn statement made by Mathilda Hayton, the youngest of the two children at the heart of the case, she has never privately nor publicly gone back on what was claimed at the time of the hearing. Neither Mathilda nor her brother had a history of mental illness, and neither I nor my colleagues have been able to find any symptoms that might indicate delusion.

I have gathered together some of the clinical case material* that was compiled in the months before the trial. They are a record of interviews and statements made by the children following their father's arrest. I have also included the celebrated letters obtained by Graham Hayton as part of his investigation and purport to throw light on the testimony of Mathilda.

Dr Jay Carter of the University of Cambridge has stated that they are documents consistent with what is now known to have taken place in the immediate environs of New Barton.

Inevitably, I have received help and advice from a number of colleagues, and I would like to offer my thanks to Peter Westbrook and Catherine Heller of the Department of Psychology at the University of Southampton and to Dr Gwyneth James of St Margaret's Hospital.

**See Note on the text*

I am indebted to Brian and Kate Hayton, Violet Thompson and Keith Pyatt for their cooperation.

Theresa Davies
June 2001

Note on the text

The main body of the text is provided by Graham Hayton. He worked on this narrative, with the help of David Lincoln from the firm William Scheiffer and Son. Graham made use of notes and tapes compiled at the time of the legal proceedings and has attempted, in his own words, 'to tell what happened using only the evidence of my experience.'

Mathilda's contribution is more fragmentary. The conversations were recorded over a period of weeks and I have simply transcribed the interviews using conventional notation (that is, underlining shows emphasis; square brackets indicate sounds that can't be easily transcribed and so on).

It is worth observing that during the period of conversation, Mathilda sometimes found it difficult to put her thoughts into words – either because of her immaturity or because of the emotional upset occasioned by the trial. However, her account is never less than compelling. And, as ever, corroborates the statements of her brother.

The narratives have been interleaved for convenience. In some instances they duplicate each other; at other times they are an additional witness.

Graham did not have access to his sister's statements, before or after the trial proceedings. Nor did he read the transcripts whilst engaged in compiling his version of events.

TD

One

TD/MH: 19.4.99

0001–0040

MH —my name is Mathilda Emily Hayton and I live at Sentinel House Potters Road New Barton (.) I'm five years old and my phone number is New Barton 738911

TD —my goodness Mathilda (.) that's a lot of information

(2)

TD —you're working on a painting

(3)

TD —that's a very big house

(3)

TD —is that your house (.)

MH —yes (.)

TD —who lives in the house with you

(2)

TD —who's in your family (.)

MH —mummy (.) and my daddy

(3)

TD —anyone else (.) is there anyone else in your family

(2)

TD —do you have a brother (.)

MH —Graham (1)

TD —I thought so (1) can you tell me how old Graham is (.)

MH —Graham is ah fifteen (.)

TD —thank you (.) that was very helpful (.) can we look at your painting again

(2)

TD —what's that next to the house (.)

MH —those are trees (.) there's a path over there as well but the trees er cover the path (.)

TD —is that a kind of a ah lighthouse (.)

MH —no (.) that's a ro- ro- rocket (.)

TD —my goodness (.) you have a rocket on your front lawn (.)

MH —it's a pretend rocket (.) my daddy works on rockets when he goes to the office (.) that's his job (.)

TD —he's a rocket man

(3)

TD —right (.) and you've got some more trees there (.) and a car (1) what's that looking out from the window there

(2)

TD —is that a member of the family (.)

MH —that's [inaudible] (1)

TD —I'm sorry (.) I didn't hear what you said (.)

MH —ghost (.)

TD —uh ah a ghost (1)

TD —is that a pretend ghost

(2)

TD —Mathilda (.) I was asking

MH —no (.) the ghost is in the house (.) <u>with us</u>

(2)

MH —it's real [crying]

Two

It was a terrible day. Last autumn. The first leaves curling over and three of us depressed.

We'd left Dad in the kitchen, the mobile jammed to his ear, and joined the trail of removal guys humping boxes down the drive. Waiting patiently by the tailgate as bits of our lives were taken and shoved in position in that dark cavern. All the while Dad yelling abuse at Margaret Samuels, his personal assistant at Spere.

Matty was most concerned with her soft toy collection, I recall, and mum had taken responsibility for fragile stuff – glass knick-knacks, ornaments, that kind of thing.

Removal day.

There's so much more to it than simply shifting stuff from one place to the next. I'd spent my life in Nether Ashton. Been to school there. Learnt to translate pencil squiggles into awesome graffiti in the boys' toilets. Learnt to ride a bike without gripping the handlebars. Learnt to know the difference between a V-sign with palm facing outwards and the other variety.

But this isn't a nostalgia-trip.

Let's hear from the big man:

'No. NO! I don't mean that, Margaret. That is positively NOT what I want. Look. Can you get on to Canine Video immediately and spell out the specifications? What? No, NO. Will you listen to me for at least three seconds? Yeah yeah. I know that. I was the person who vetoed the decision in the first place. Look, Margaret. Believe me . . . yes. Yes . . .'

The thing about Dad was that he was always so intense about work. I don't remember when the mobile first entered his life, but believe me, it didn't make anything one bit easier. Not for him. Not for Mum. Not for any of us. It was like a portable stress machine. Whenever that little bleeper went you could see the physical change that came over Dad. His shoulders would tense. He would lose any smile that was trying to find a way on to his face. He was immediately on all points alert.

Matty used to say that he'd got his Mr McGregor face on, after the gardener in that book by Beatrix Potter, but I felt he looked messed up. The way I've seen quite a few teachers who work in our school.

Technology was his life. It could have been his death. But that was later on.

It was a bad moment for Margaret Samuels to call because Dad had been busy supervising the removal guys – ensuring that the stuff was shifted in the right order, racing around to see that he'd put messages on all the boxes – you know, KITCHEN and SECOND BEDROOM lettered in bright red.

The one category that Dad wasn't trusting to the delivery people were the three that he'd marked STUDY. That was because as soon as we 'touched base', as he put it, he intended to leap out of the car, with a box under one arm and the keys in his spare hand, and open the house and immediately (I kid you not) start getting the fax machine plugged in and the computer wired up and so on and so forth. The whole bit.

This removal business made him insecure, I think. Not the actual departure from a home, but temporary disconnection from the Mother Ship. I don't think he could conceive of effective communication without 240 volts and a dozen buttons to punch. So, our home was packed up and put away and after a last-minute sandwich, we were in the car and heading south.

It was gone 3.30 and being mid-October the sun was drifting towards the horizon. Matty had her eyes closed, listening to Roald Dahl, and Mum had her face stuffed into a Stephen King horror story. Periodically, Dad would turn on the radio and then channel hop until Mum gave him the verbal.

'We're just going over the escarpment now children,' said Dad presently. This was a smart word for hill, but I was the only one tuned in to his travelogue.

'What do you notice about the vegetation up here?' he asked after a while. It was a question directed at me, because

Mum was meeting the devil in Castle Rock and Matty was in some other space-time continuum.

'There's not much?' I guessed, looking at the scrubby grass and wind-bent trees.

'Correct. Ten points,' said Dad. 'Why's that, do you wonder?'

And it was whilst I was reflecting on why there wasn't Amazonian rainforest covering this part of southern England that the first threads of mist started to drift across the road.

And very soon, like after two hundred metres, from being a pleasant late autumn afternoon, we were driving into a cloudbank. Dad stopped his interrogation and Mum put aside her text.

'This is a surprise,' she said, as Dad cut his speed so that we were crawling at about twenty mph. You couldn't see anything in front except the yellow of the car's beam. It was like a great hand was pushing on the sky to suffocate the world.

'Do you think you should put your hazard warners on?' asked Mum after a while.

There was a long pause as we inched ahead. The only sound being the low rumble of the engine and crunch-crunch of the tyres on the road surface.

'Maybe,' said Dad, leaning forward and peering into the grey murk. 'It's not getting any clearer, and that's for sure.'

In a weird way it was like the whole world had been erased and we were left cautiously patrolling an alien landscape. Nothing in front; nothing behind. No trees, no stars, no people.

At which point, Mum jolted Matty awake with the exclamation. 'What's that? There. Up ahead.'

To begin with, I couldn't make anything out in the great shifting nothingness, but then, taking form out of the fog was the shadow and then the substance of a man. He was standing right in the middle of the road, his legs astride and his right arm pushed out against us, the flat of his hand upraised. It said: stop. It said: go no further.

Three

'YeeaaAHHHH!'

Was the sound that woke me when Dad got the news about the house down at New Barton.

It was a Saturday morning, naturally, because on a weekday he's out of the place like a whirlwind and on the road, dictating notes, by 7.30.

'We've got it, Kate!' yelled Dad again, loud enough to unsettle the pigeons that were resting in the tree outside my room.

'Very good Brian,' said Kate obediently.

And then: 'Daddy – Daddy? Was that, was that – the dark house? Jenny said it was – ah – it had a ghost.'

Silence.

The pigeons fluttered back to their post and I picked up my glasses from the bedside table.

'Well, I think Jenny is being a bit silly, Matty,' I could imagine him picking her up and putting her on his knee. 'It was a funny old house, wasn't it? Creaking and groooaaannniiiing!'

Matty giggled into her hands.

'I expect you'll creak and groan when you're a hundred and fifty-eight.'

And she laughed again and then: 'Don't!' she shrieked. 'It tickles. Don't Daddeee!'

I then heard the disgusting smacking noise that meant he'd given her a kiss.

She laughed, struggled – and he must have put her down, because the next thing there's a rush of her feet on the landing and her red face has peered round the door of my room.

'Graham?' she said, coming to my bedside.

'I heard,' I said. 'We're moving into the New Barton house.'

'Yes,' she replied, sitting on the bed and looking towards the window. Then really quietly: 'I was frightened. By the noises. Do you remember Graham?'

Yes. I remembered. Of all the three zillion properties we'd been dragged around, this was the one that looked as though it had been designed by the makers of a horror film. You know: double gates at the road, a short gravelled drive, porch, exposed woodwork, double-fronted. Dark.

The owners had already slipped off to some place in the sun when we took a look round, so we were left with the energetic Mr Pierpoint to do the tedious business of emphasising the good and concealing the bad.

The previous owners, the two Misses Winter, were great conservers of electricity, so every room was lit with the glow of 60-watt bulbs. I'm not fooling, but when I came out of that place, I had a headache that banged like a pneumatic drill.

Matty sat on the bed, looking at my book on steam engines. She flicked the pages and then said: 'Graham, does the new house – the one we went to – have a ghost inside?'

The kind thing to tell a five-year-old was no, of course not; you only find ghosts in films and books, but then I wasn't sure. So I said: 'I expect the house is just old, like Dad says. You know, the timber and pipes and stuff aren't properly insulated.'

'But it felt, it felt funny,' she went on, looking up from the book.

It *had* felt funny. And that wasn't the only thing: whilst we'd been there, clustered together in one of the first floor bedrooms, and as Mr Pierpoint was describing the features ('You can see that even the glass in the windows is original, Mrs Hayton. Imagine, we're looking through the panes that people dozens of years ago looked through'), there was a fizzing noise from the single bulb and we were then dropped into a grey half-light.

No one said anything for a second or two; I think we were all surprised by the interference of something unplanned, but then Mr P was able to make some comment about the bulbs being original features too, and we shuffled off to look at something else.

So I said to Matty: 'Look, sometimes our senses play tricks on us. You think something is a bit odd, but really it's your imagination putting all sorts of strange ideas into your head.'

'OK,' she said at last. 'But that house doesn't seem' – she looked around the room for a moment – 'friendly' and she slid off the bed and wandered away.

'What's going on mate?'

Dad had lowered his window and was calling to the figure in the road.

He didn't move, didn't say anything.

'You know,' said Mum, 'he's a soldier. Look. I'm sure he's wearing a helmet and that's webbing or whatever you call it strapped to his body.'

She was right, of course. Because now she'd given a label to his occupation, we could detect the traces of uniform, imagine the khaki cloth.

'Probably on manoeuvres,' said Dad, picking up his phone and punching in the usual machine-gun tap of numbers.

As he sat listening to the receiver, we all heard, faintly at first, but growing louder as it got closer, the slow clinking and clanking of machinery. And then, inching up and on to the road behind the soldier, the dark outline of a tracked vehicle.

None of us spoke. The soldier didn't turn round or deviate from his station, and the tank made its painful progress from one verge to the next; its great caterpillar tracks pulling its lozenge of dark brown, as if a huge clod of earth had decided to cut its ties with the ground and go exploring.

'Of course, the weather has messed up the reception,'

said Dad, switching off the phone. 'If it carries on like this, we might as well check into a hotel for the night.' He watched the slow passage of the army up ahead.

He looked at his watch. 'My goodness,' he said, 'it's taken us an hour to cover thirty-five miles.'

As he spoke, the vehicle vanished as completely as a pebble dropped into a pond, leaving behind a falling cloud of exhaust and the soldier. He turned to his left, and walked back into the dark.

After that, as we moved ahead, the weather improved and soon we could see the road stretching to the next hill.

We stopped at a café before Salisbury and it was already dark by the time we passed through the village of Brenton Underwood and saw the name plate that announced the hamlet of New Barton.

Sentinel House is beyond the other buildings, on the right-hand side. Our headlights caught the old gate as we slowly patrolled the single lane track. They also picked up the heavy chain and padlock that secured the entrance.

'Now what?' said Dad, once more giving in to his well developed sense of frustration. 'I suppose it's back to Salisbury to get the key so that we can unlock the gate to get into the yard to gain access to the house.'

'There isn't a key on the bunch Mr Pierpoint gave you?'

'Why should there be?' asked Dad, his voice rising in tone. 'There was no mention of a padlock or chains when we made the arrangement to move in. This is supposed to be a home not a prison.'

Nor a nightmare, I thought. But by this time, I felt it was probably worthwhile leaving Mum and Dad to shout out their differences. There was a torch in the front glove compartment and so I persuaded a reluctant Matty to come with me and explore.

We crossed the road and climbed over the gate. Beyond the trees and bushes we entered a place of silence. The house was outlined against the lighter blue of the night sky and it sat there, mute, heavy and solid. Like some strange animal staring at us through the empty black holes of its eyes.

'I don't like this,' said Matty. And then, tugging at my hand, 'Let's go back.'

I turned and looked over at the car. They had the interior light on by this time and Dad was busy with the phone.

I switched on the torch, its thin beam picking up the tufts of grass growing through the gravel. 'No,' I said, 'Let's go and and see what we can find.'

We walked on three or four paces, and I stopped. 'You know, it may be a bit scary Matty, but there's nothing here to hurt us.'

I'm not sure I believed my own reassurance, but I think a trace of conviction in my voice got through to her. She squeezed my hand and we walked up to the entrance, my torch flicking across the dust-covered windows of the empty rooms. The door was, predictably, locked, and so we stepped across the front towards the side gate that led to the garden at the back.

I'd just put my hand on the latch, had just touched the cold metal when a great face, all slavering teeth and dark eyes leapt up out of the darkness and roared its fury at us.

Four

I dreamt of Dad that night.

We were walking up a grassy slope, he slightly ahead of me. It felt like early morning because the grass was wet. You could feel the cold of autumn and there was the drone of cars on a main road.

The next moment we're standing beside one of the huge support chains that hold up the roadway on the Clifton bridge in Bristol. I could see the stone tower of the upright rising into the mist. Dad stood by the chain, legs astride, wavy brown hair neatly parted.

He pointed behind him and said, his voice clear and confident: 'This is the direct route to the best view in Bristol. Follow me to the top.' And he turned and leaning forward, stepped onto the chain and started his ascent, one foot in front of the other.

At one point, he paused and looked over his shoulder. He shouted: 'Don't look down. It's really clear up here.'

Then he reached the mist and vanished. Not a trace.

Then I've woken in a strange room.

There was grey light dribbling in from the blanket I'd pinned against the window, and I could make out my clothes and stuff heaped in a pile on the floor.

As the dream seeped away I was left thinking about the incident that had frightened Matty so much that it was to be an age before she was able to calm down and control her breathing – that strange meeting at the gated corner of the house.

The thing was, neither of us heard anything to warn us of what was going to leap out of that darkness. The open jaws and the great roaring barks split the night like an axe.

It wasn't any good the voice that followed it – 'There Joey, come on, good dog. Come on boy' – because Matty had run back to the main gate and was already heaving herself over.

'Hello my dear,' said the figure, emerging from the shadow of the house. In the torchlight I could see that he was a bit older than Dad, was wearing a brown flat cap and duffle coat. 'You must be the family that's about to move in.'

It wasn't a question. He opened the side gate and all I could do was nod.

'I'm David Thomas,' he went on, holding the lead on the now-silent labrador. 'Sorry to give you and your sister a bit of a fright. The thing is, there was a whisper in the village that some travellers were seen in the grounds about here and I've been coming over each day to check for squatters. Last thing you want when you're going to move in.'

Dad was climbing over the front gate by this time, and when we reached him, Mr Thomas explained what had happened. He went over to the chain that had prevented the family's entrance and pulled open the lock.

'It's just a deterrent,' he said. 'I never shut the clasp so you could've just opened her up and driven on in. The removal people have been and gone an hour since.'

He was a softly spoken man and the Welsh voice added to the odd feel of the night. Like waking up in a house affected by subsidence: everything seemed slightly out of joint – the world was still there, but changed.

Which again was like Mr Thomas's face. I wasn't really aware of it then, but later it was obvious that he didn't have full control of his facial muscles, so that instead of his features balancing, the left-hand side was pulled down, almost as if an invisible hand had grabbed hold of the skin and flesh beneath his chin and tugged hard. This exposed the lower lid of his eye, so that on cold days it seemed to fill up and water almost as if he were crying with some private sadness.

'Heard you were a computer man, Mr Hayton,' he continued, blind to Dad's evident desire to get in and switch on the real world. 'Got a PC myself. Use it for games mainly, you understand. Do you play games at all? No, well I expect you'd be too busy.

'Just got a word-processing package and one of them things you use to send letters by the telephone—'

'Modem,' said Dad sadly, turning to look back as

Mum brought Matty out of the car.

'Modem!' said Mr Thomas. 'Modem. That's the Jimmy as my mam would say. Perhaps I could pay you a call – when you've got settled in like – and you might show me how a "modem" actually works? Not that I've got anyone to send messages to, mind.'

And with that, he opened the double gates, and waved himself off into the night.

We didn't do a lot of unpacking when we got in. The house was bitterly cold and as before haunted by strange echoes and odd sounds. It took Dad fifteen minutes to find the boiler and then another ten to work out how to get the pilot light started. I was surprised that he hadn't plugged in the computer and asked for help on the internet.

We spent the next week, the week of half-term, 'creating the familial infrastructure' as Mum put it (i.e. unpacking and cleaning and shifting stuff around).

Matty and myself were given the opportunity to help out before we were dropped into our new schools, and Dad, well, once the study was wired and ready to go, he just carried on starting early and working late. He didn't leave at 7.30 to begin with, but then a major American client became interested in the software Dad's company were producing for StarRaider, so he was rarely seen during daylight hours.

Sometimes there would be a sudden flare-up at Dad's time-keeping and you'd hear raised voices and accusations late in the night. The point being that we'd moved to be nearer the office, not to continue with former habits.

But this isn't a tale of marital strife, as my English teacher Miss Crowther would put it, and I don't want to get too unfocused (as she would also point out).

So we'll skip the traumas of new school and zip the clock forward three weeks. We're late-November now. The leaves have done their autumn stuff and I had learnt the complications of the Year 10 timetable. Dad was absent for vast swathes of time and Mum was decorating the attic room.

The first odd thing I noticed as I trudged up the lane that Friday afternoon was that there was this guy in the middle of the road, under the streetlight, playing with a ball – lifting it in the air with his foot, using his thighs to keep it aloft.

When I got closer I could see he was about my age – light brown hair, freckles, red sweatshirt, jeans.

He didn't take much notice until I was about to go past him to get to the gate when he nodded the ball into his hands and turned to me.

'Watcha,' he said, smiling, and I noticed his front tooth was chipped.

'Hi,' I said.

'Moved into the house?' he asked, the ball now tucked under his arm.

'Yes,' I stopped, and close to I could see that his hair had a slight orange tinge, so that the overall effect was like a chestnut colour. Auburn I expect Mum would have said. And he had a clear south Wilts accent: the 'r' sounds were stressed so that 'watcha' was more 'watcherr' if you can imagine that.

'Been empty for over a year,' he said, looking over the wall at the house. 'Been inside a few times myself. On and off.'

'Yes?'

'Ye-es. Dad did some work for the Winter sisters. You know, plumbing, painting, that sort of touch.'

He dropped the ball to his feet and kicked it against the wall.

'Seen you at school. You're in Armitage's group.'

'That's right.' Yet I couldn't place this confident face now concentrating on tapping the ball against the brickwork.

'I've seen you a few times. On the bus and that. Catch it before you. By the shop.'

'Right.'

He paused. 'So. Have you got a bike then? A set of wheels?' He looked at me, smiling.

'Yes. Nothing special.'

'That's OK, then,' and he lifted the ball in the air, heading the return onto the road. 'I'll give you a call. I'm John Franklin,' and he trotted off, tapping the ball from side to side.

'I'm Graham Hayton,' I called after him.

'I know,' he said. 'See you.'

The second surprise was to find the Toyota sitting out

the front. It might have been just a car to John, but to me it meant that Dad was home and it hadn't turned four o'clock.

As expected he was sitting in the study tapping away, but as soon as he heard the front door open, he stopped and came out.

'Graham!' he said.

'Right,' I said. 'I live here. Who are you?'

'Of course!' he replied. 'Anyway, I've had a great day at work and – how did you get on by the way?'

'Oh fine Dad, fine, got caned a couple of times and there was a fatal stabbing during the lunch break, but otherwise it was A-1.'

'Right!' and he laughed in that great open-handed way of his, eyes twinkling. And then, as I followed him down the hall, 'It looks as though we're ninety-seven per cent certain of picking up the Douglas-Knight contract for our software.'

'Is that the American deal you were so interested in?' I replied. The thing being, if you've got a father who's a senior programmer for a large company, it's quite easy to lose track of the occasional successes he achieved.

'They're sending a team over in a couple of weeks' time and I'm going to share the presentation.'

'Is that like a special talk?' I asked, imagining something like school assembly going on forever.

'Yes, that kind of thing.' He smiled, smoothing his hair. 'You see the purpose of the visit is to show some pretty shrewd cookies what our technology can do and why they should buy it.'

'But I didn't think StarRaider was flying yet?' I asked him.

'Well, there's what's known as a pre-prototype that we're using to test the avionics and so on. Anyhow, after tea, I'll show you something that will . . . will—'

'Blow my mind?'

'Well, possibly,' and he laughed again as he turned the tap to fill the kettle. His wide-eyed enthusiasm was touching: he was like a ten-year-old who'd just been picked to captain the first eleven.

Mum was out with Matty sorting out the groceries at the supermarket, so I went upstairs and put *Viron* through its paces. If you've got one of the current games machines, then this 32-bit 'shoot 'em up' experience will seem like so much junk, but if you needed to let off steam, to fire and destroy incoming marauders, then it was the perfect end to another day at school.

I had never actually got much further along the line than the multi-gun laser fortress, but today I seemed to have lucked in and I was annihilating the opposition like I was the captain of a helicopter gunship.

Dad had come up the stairs at some stage and I knew that he was standing behind me, looking down at the screen, but with three lives to go and 348,000 points showing, there wasn't time to discuss the latest triumph of the world's foremost computer expert.

‘YES!’ I said as one of the immunity bubbles appeared and I was able to trigger a local nuclear holocaust.

In the space it took for the new landscape to form, I took a quick look to acknowledge Dad’s presence; to say ‘Hi’.

He wasn’t there, of course. Just the long corridor, the worn carpet and the dark pattern of the stained-glass window above the stairs.

Five

'From out of the darkness
tumbling and turning
vapour rising from the upper surfaces
a scream of the future.

Cruising low over a forested plain
firing up into a vertical climb
contrails forming from the reheat of the engines
sunlight flashing on the light, on the flame
of the glistening cockpit curve.

The StarRaider

That shiny, sleek, shark-finned glimpse of the quick
the magical flick and roll of the jet plane
crossing and diving the ever-so-blue, ever-so-deadly sky.

Blasting at unseen foes
guided by heat
by the radar blip

by the touch of a button
and then
the rush and the flame
of the grey gunmetal flash
that surf these climbs
to impact with a gasp
of orange and black on some long-gone spot
dropping away from the blue.'

We sat in the study. Listening to the voice-over; staring at a blank screen before we saw sunlight flashing up over the dark curve of the Earth and then the sudden shock of a high speed aircraft roaring past at maybe 30,000 feet.

Although I'm not exactly in love with the military, I recognised that this was footage of the new plane. We saw it rifling into a climb; coming in at road height; rolling away from a pursuit plane and firing a missile at an invisible target.

It was hugely entertaining, believe me, like enjoying a switchback ride from the vantage point of a camera strapped to the front. Or watching a carefully edited sequence from an air combat movie. The commentary supplied all the vital statistics: whether it was details relating to endurance or the facts about its service ceiling.

Everything was hard and clear, and sitting with the rest of the family, I felt the reassurance and warmth of our shared lives. Matty had her head tilted to one side and Mum was holding the broken frame of her specs in position so that she could follow the sequence. Dad stood to my left, the TV control in his right hand, obviously well-pleased with the demonstration. I could hear him humming his satisfaction as images of the diving, swerving marvel were projected onto the lenses of his glasses.

And yet for a few seconds earlier on, I had felt the foundations of my life shift and turn; like my world was rotating on castors. For I *had* heard someone and I *had* felt their presence behind me. And furthermore, I knew they were *so* close they had been pressing into the upright of my study chair. From that moment I was convinced that we weren't alone in the house and that whatever else happened, we were unlikely to remain alone.

Then Matty's voice dragged me back into the study: 'Daddy – what does your plane *do*? Does it take people away – like – on holiday?'

'Not quite, Matt,' he said. 'Let me explain,' and he went over and sat on the coffee table in front of her. 'It's what we call a *combat* aircraft. You see, if enemies come over a country to drop bombs on houses and families, then this aeroplane can go up and stop them from doing that.'

'And how good is it?' I asked.

'The greatest leap forward in aviation technology since Reginald Mitchell decided on elliptical wings for the Spitfire,' he said, and I could tell that he was now quoting from some invisible sales brochure. Like he was using us to rehearse his special promotion's spiel.

'What you have just seen is a machine that will fill order

books and line runways wherever there's a country that needs aircraft that are both low cost and high performance.

'And what makes that little beauty buzz, what makes it twist and turn and soar like a bird (and yet what bird can fly like that?) is contained in the latest fly-by-wire technology stored in the binary code of the plane's onboard computers. Without them,' and he paused, to allow all this stuff to sink in, 'the craft drops out of the sky, unstable, unflyable even. But with the constant flow of electronic information, the digital dots and dashes transform twelve tons of hardware into a trans-sonic precision tool.

'This little beauty can detect and knock out a target smaller than my hand from a distance of over one hundred miles.

'This little beauty, using the latest satellite decoder, can be placed on to the slipstream of a target that isn't even *within* radar range.

'And this little tool is kept aloft, twisting and turning by the binary codes contained in two three-and-a-half inch disks. Imagine: from only three point two megs of instructions and you've got a machine that can cruise the stratosphere at over two and a half times the speed of sound'.

He turned round, flicked the catches on his case and produced a pair of computer disks. They looked pretty standard to me and, except for the red strip running along the bottom, they could be the kind of thing possessed by several hundred million households.

'These are the disks that contain the essential information

for the aircraft,' he said. 'The bits of plastic that keep me running late at the office.'

'So, so, those disks, or rather what's on them, is valuable?' I asked.

'Well, put it like this,' said Dad. 'There's fifteen years' work gone into this software. So you can calculate for yourself that these applications are worth more than a week's pocket money.'

'But,' I went on, 'well then, isn't it dangerous to go walking around the place with them? You might be mugged or we could be burgled.'

'Yes, there is that possibility. There is such a thing as industrial espionage, but (a) I hardly ever remove them from the office and (b) if they are being transported, they're kept in this' – and he pointed to his case – 'which has reinforced steel sides and is secured by a Dragon Code lock.'

'But you must have copies of the software at work?'

'Oh yes,' said Dad. 'But we still wouldn't like the knowledge to become widely available.'

At which point Matty's tinny voice piped up from the depths of her chair.

She said: 'Is your plane made for killing people?'

It was like Dad had just taken a fast ball from left field. His mouth hung half-open and he reached over to hang on to the computer monitor on his desk as if to steady his balance.

'Well,' he began, pushing his glasses up to rub his eyes. 'Well.'

'But what happens,' she said, 'what happens if the – ah – enemies buy the aeroplane? Won't they use it – to kill other people?'

Again, Dad seemed to be stranded, as if the smooth speedboat of the salesman had suddenly beached on a sand dune that had no right to be in the main channel.

He sighed. We watched.

'I suppose that could happen,' he admitted. 'It's a possibility. Sure. But the government sorts out who should get planes like this, and if they think the country that wants to buy the equipment is bad, then the sale will be prevented.'

'But the aeroplane will *kill* people?'

'Look. Don't let's get into that again,' said Dad. 'It's a very complicated issue, and well, let's leave that for another day.'

'But daddeee,' she persisted. 'Mrs Jones told us a story about Jesus and she said that it was' – her brow furrowed with effort – 'she said it was wrong to kill people. She said' – and again Matty paused, trying to extract the crucial piece of information from wherever it was stored.

'Well, you tell me what Mrs Jones said when you remember it dear,' said Dad, pushing the videotape back into its box and opening his silky smooth black case.

'Jesus said you've got to *love* your enemies!' It all came out in one great excited rush. It had been the equivalent of carrying a heavy box up a flight of stairs, but Matty had worked at it and worried at it and when she laid her idea on the table, I think she knew that she had presented Dad with an unexploded bomb.

Looking back at it now, with June sunlight pouring into my bedroom, it seems like Matty hadn't been overwhelmed by the video and the polished talk; that she was asking all the right questions in her own naive way.

And other ears heard.

And other eyes watched.

He didn't reply at first and Mum went out to start clearing up the kitchen. I could hear her stacking plates and letting the water run hot.

But eventually, like when the silence had got really uncomfortable, he turned round and sat down on one of the armchairs.

'This is really complicated stuff,' he said, his eyes dark, his brows raised. 'You're asking me very tough questions. Because, at the end of the day, my company does develop products that are used in aircraft that have been used to kill people. There's no running away from that fact.

'But I also bring home a salary that helps pay for the house and the car and the nice things. And pays for the holidays that we have, and so on.

'I'm aware of what Jesus said, Matty. I'm not a religious man, but like everyone else, I'm trying to do my best for all of us.'

Quite frankly I was surprised that he'd taken the whole thing so seriously. Usually with Dad a serious question got a jokey answer. Or a straightforward lie. But here he was being pinned down by a five-year-old who was quoting the Bible at him.

She didn't pursue her curiosity. I don't suppose she had any more questions to ask, but I got to feeling that Dad wouldn't be given such a grilling when the faces turned up from Douglas-Knight.

I went to bed early and read an old American crime novel – where the crimes were obvious and the bad guys painted in bold colours. There was something comforting in this made-up world because you knew that the villains were going to get put away and the private detective would get the girl. And best of all, you didn't have to puzzle out who to side with.

I don't remember turning out the light, but the next thing I recall was Matty anxiously, terrifyingly, tugging me awake. For outside, down below, next to the house, stamping their feet in unison over the gravel, was the sound of marching men.

Six

TD/MH: 26.4.99

0001–0040

TD —hello (.) how are you today

(2)

TD —did you see TV over the weekend (.) There was a good film on Saturday

(2)

TD —the last time I saw you we had a look at the painting you had done at school (.) do you remember (.)

MH —it was the house picture (.)

TD —it was the house picture (.) you told me about the rocket and the trees and the path (.) do you remember

MH —[Inaudible]

TD —I'm sorry (.) I didn't catch

MH —the ghost

TD —yes that's right (.) you showed the ghost looking out of the window (.)

MH —he was looking at me (.)

TD —he was looking at you (.)

MH —yes (.)

TD —does the ghost live in the house

(2)

TD —do you know who it is

(3)

TD —but you've seen him (.)

MH —you can hear him moving around sometimes (.)

TD —but you don't know his name (.)

MH —he's not as old as daddy(.)

TD —did he live in the house (.)

MH —it wasn't his house (2) he stayed there (.)

TD —was this a long time ago Matty (1) did he stay in the house over a hundred years ago (.)

MH —he didn't want to stay in the house (.)

TD —was he unhappy in the house

MH —[Inaudible]

TD —I didn't catch that (.)

MH —he (.) he was alone (.) he didn't have friends (.) he was lonely (.) he had no one to help him he had no one to talk to

(2)

—he was in great (1) he was in danger

(2)

—he didn't want to die (1)

TD —were there people who were hurting him in the house (1) Matty (.)

MH —he said though I walk through the valley of the shadow of death I will fear no evil for thou art with me thy rod and thy staff they comfort me (.)

Seven

The morning after the marching incident I sat opposite Mum at the breakfast table, watching her take a bone-handled knife and carefully slice the top off a boiled egg.

'Did you get back to sleep?' she asked after a while.

I nodded. My mouth was full of cereal.

'I'm going to let Matty sleep in,' she said. 'She was awake until gone three.'

'You said you never heard the noise?' I asked.

She shook her head. 'You know me, sleep through a hydrogen bomb.'

What *had* woken Mum and Dad was the sound of Matty's screams from my room, but by the time the light was on and my parents had arrived, the marching had gone and all you could hear was Matty's muffled sobs.

I explained to Mum and Dad what I'd heard, but what kind of sense can you make of a fifteen-year-old who talks about the sound of marching feet in the middle of the night? In the broad light of day, with Mum eating her way through a boiled egg and toast, and with a blackbird calling in the garden, the world seemed peaceful and calm. But in the dark, in a house full of odd sounds and whispers and with the unmistakable tramp tramp tramp of marching feet, everything seemed strange and threatening and sinister.

Dad pulled back the curtain to look outside, but with the exception of shadows thrown across the garden from the window, there was nothing mysterious in the dark.

'An aural mirage,' he said after a moment, and yawned. 'It's to do with the density of the air. Like you can hear trains from quite a distance when it's a clear night, well similarly other sound travels.'

I thought about it for a moment. The red alarm clock on my shelf said 12.40.

'But Dad, who would be having a parade at a little after midnight?'

He shrugged. 'Who knows? There's all sorts of army camps and bases and stuff around here. Why, you remember that tank we met on our way down?'

So, midnight manoeuvres it was.

After a while, I said to Mum: 'Do you think this house is haunted?'

She looked at me quickly and then wiped her mouth with a tissue.

'I think people sometimes put together different kinds of information and perhaps come to the conclusion that there are ghosts or whatnot in a building or place. Usually, they're old houses and very rarely inner city flats or new developments. And why is that do you think?'

'Because old places have more of an atmosphere?'

'Yes,' she said. 'And because, as Dad said the other day, they tend to groan and creak more than new places. And also, everyone has seen ghost films and so forth on television. So when it's dark and creepy, we probably imagine more.'

'I did hear the sound Mum,' I said firmly. 'I don't know whether I was listening to the ghosts of men marching or that mirage thing Dad was talking about, but what Matty heard, I heard also.'

And there was something else, something I hadn't spoken about. When I woke up there was writing on the window.

Being a Saturday, it was a little after ten to nine and I'd got up to see if there was a trace of the phantom soldiers. As I pulled back the curtain, I saw that someone had written in the condensation that clung to the pane. The letters spelt: 'Gas . . .'

There was obviously more, but the curtain had caught the glass as I'd dragged it back so all that was left was a word that didn't seem to go anywhere.

'If,' I began, distracting Mum from her newspaper. 'If there were such things as ghosts, what do you think they mean?'

'Well,' she began, and then added, 'you'll have to accept Graham that I don't believe for one minute in the existence of ghosts, but given that, then I suppose you might put together some reason for their activities. Some people have said they're the spirits of tormented people who remain in the area where they suffered. Or you could argue that they're unhappy spirits who have a message for the living.

'In *Hamlet*, the ghost has . . .'

But she lost me at that point. She used to teach at a college and, give her half a chance, she'd be treading the boards as a lecturer again. I suppose chatting to Mum *was* comforting, but her reasonable voice didn't quite push away the fear of the night.

At which point, there was a loud rap on the kitchen door behind me. The kind of noise that might announce the arrival of the local police with a warrant to search the house.

'That's loud enough to wake the dead,' said Mum, smiling.

Bang.

Bang.

Bang.

I got the ancient key and turned the lock. The key in the lock of the door that opened up to the serious face of John Franklin.

'Hi,' he said. 'My bike's out the front.'

'Oh, right,' I replied.

After I'd done all the introductions and stuff, got my coat and said I'd be back in time for lunch etcetera etcetera, I pulled my bike from the shed and walked with John to the road.

'Got settled in then?' he asked as we stood outside the gate.

'Oh yes,' I said. 'Just about unpacked my gear.'

'Bit quiet for you perhaps?'

'No. We lived in a village in the north of the county and that didn't have a main road near it.'

'Oh you're well set up here then,' and he stared back at the house, the suggestion of a smile touching the corners of his mouth. It was like there was some joke that he knew about but which he didn't intend to share. Some secret knowledge.

'Have you been to Wilson's Wood?' he asked after I'd closed the gate.

And when I told him I hadn't even heard of the place, he said: 'Right. Let's go then,' and shot off, out of New Barton in the direction of Craybourne. For a Saturday morning ride, he set a cracking pace. We went for about a mile, and I was glad that I'd worn my jacket, because it started to rain after ten minutes, being carried by a stiff wind slanting in from the right so that I was soon soaked.

Eventually, we came to a line of poplars that crossed the road and John swung left on to the tree-lined track that climbed the hill.

He stopped and waited for me to catch up.

'There's a track round the wood,' he said. 'Like cycle-cross. Plenty of ramps and bumps to ride up over. Plenty of mud and water too.' He grinned.

The track between the avenue of poplars was rutted and puddled and used by vehicles of some sort, and horses too. Their hoof-marks were printed out clearly in the pale earth. The green line of the wood could be seen rising over the brow of the hill, and when we reached it I was glad to pause to catch my breath.

Once amongst the trees, it grew dark – the grey light falling onto the brown track that went off at right angles up ahead of us.

'If we go down thataways,' said John pointing to the left, 'we'll come to the clearing and the huts. We'll go and have a look see.'

'Right,' I said, wiping the rain from my glasses. 'What huts?'

'You'll see,' he said and pushed off, standing up to force speed from his back wheel.

The track was obviously used by vehicles for taking away felled trees or something. There were plenty of tyre marks in the mud and puddles that looked deceptively shallow. I dropped abruptly into one and only just kept my balance, a brown slurry rising up my legs.

But John never stopped, never faltered. Through the grey mist of my smeared and wet glasses, I could see him in front, head down and pushing away.

The track swung in a gentle curve to the right, and I could make out a spur from the main route and some kind of fence in the distance. As we got closer I could see the shapes of several long huts, the kind you see in military bases.

'See you got yourself a soaking,' said John when I reached him. 'And I'm froze myself,' he added. 'We can leave our bikes here and have a look at the old camp. Nothing much left, but you can find things. Like cartridge cases.'

I looked beyond him at the chain-link fencing. Someone had used the wire to string up the bodies of dead animals – stoats, weasels, rats, a squirrel. They hung there, sunken and decayed; their eye sockets pecked clean, their fur patched and thin.

Next to them, a sign on white metal:

Property of the Ministry of Defence
It is an offence to trespass on this site
KEEP OUT

'Are you sure it's OK to go in there?' I asked, a bit embarrassed by the question. Like being a five-year-old and saying: 'I don't want to get in trouble.'

Quite frankly, I've always had respect for signs that tell you to do this or not do that. I used to get hot under the collar when Mum stopped on the yellow zig-zag lines outside my old primary school. And now here we were proposing to break into a place owned by the Ministry of Defence.

I said: 'How do we get in?'

There was no obvious gate and the fence itself – crowned with rolls of barbed wire – was at least four metres high.

'Well, we're not going to pole-vault if that's what you mean,' John said, grinning. 'You're not feeling a little bit – ah – chicken, are you?' and he clucked a couple of times to demonstrate his meaning.

'Well,' I replied, avoiding his direct stare and the sarcasm of the half-raised eyebrow. 'It says it belongs to the Ministry of Defence.'

'Ministry of Defence,' he laughed and spat in the direction of the animals, wiping away a trail of spittle that hung like egg-white from his lower lip.

'We'll be OK. This place has been deserted for years. We'll hide the bikes over there, behind the bushes. Lean them up against the trees. And a bit further on, where two bits of fence meet, there's a hole we can get through.'

He smiled. 'Don't you worry. Done this thousands of times. Really.'

We propped the bikes behind some bushes and then went on for about thirty metres. Occasionally, we stopped when there was a rustle in the undergrowth – a bird or some small creature running away just to add tension to the enterprise.

The hole had been created by someone cutting through sections of wire close to the ground and then pulling back a triangle of metal. It was bent and curled over. I couldn't help wondering what hand had done this, and for what purpose. No one I knew would have had the interest or the equipment to force an entry to such a place.

But casting aside these thoughts, I followed John through, past some yew trees, to an old path that led into the camp.

It was a place of silence and decay. The grass was long and yellow, like the lank hair of an old corpse, and our feet crunched over the broken panes of scattered glass, trod uneasily over unknown mounds and bulges in the earth.

There were half a dozen huts, their windows gone, their roofs holed. There was a ramp that must have been used for vehicle inspections and the site of what had probably been a fuel depot: the vent pipes for the underground tanks were still there.

Otherwise, where the huts finished, there were just pieces of rotting wood, the ragged line of old walls, grass. It was like walking through the wreck of some sunken boat; the shapes of old life still clung about the place, but the spirit had long since gone.

When I looked round, John had disappeared.

'Hello,' I called. 'John? John!'

A pigeon clapped away from a tree beyond the fence and a piece of cloth winked from a window frame.

'Oh come on,' I called out. 'Don't be pathetic.'

The rain came down steadily and it suddenly seemed pointless to just stand in the open, getting soaked, so I made for the nearest hut, running through the mud and sodden grass.

There was no door and debris lay in piles. As I crossed the threshold, I felt the hard prod of metal and a loud voice that screamed: 'Halt! Who goes there?'

Eight

When my sight returned, I found I was on my back and staring at the broken board of an old ceiling. I could hear water dripping and smell plaster and dust. I had a headache the size of three counties and I was cold. For a moment I had difficulty in working out where I was.

Slowly, I got to a sitting position, and felt out the epicentre of pain. My hand came back stuck with blood and hair.

The hut was empty. The rain had stopped outside, but there was a cold wind blowing through the doorway. Every slow movement hurt, but once I had my head resting against the nearby wall, I could sit, with my eyes closed and wait for the tide of sickness to ebb.

Later I looked about me, checked to see that no one else was present.

The hut measured maybe 75 metres by 15. It wasn't difficult to imagine it crowded with beds and lockers; peopled with uniformed men; a stove warming the area at one end; music from a wind-up gramophone at the other.

But now, after the weather and vandals, there were

heaps of plasterboard, lager cans, yellowed newspapers and magazines. Someone had started a fire on the far side and there was an old can labelled Castrol GTX. It was the kind of place where people came to smash up or to stretch out for a desperate night's sleep.

And all comers, all visitors seem to have added to the pictures and words that covered the walls. There were crude rhymes and cartoons of women, rival football slogans and ugly scrawls about enemies and their relations.

But right next to where I sat, feeling the cool damp of the wall, was a sentence written in the style you sometimes see reproduced in history books – all loops and curls. It was neatly lettered in pencil, and it said: 'Blessed are the peacemakers: for they shall be called the children of God.'

It sounded like a kind of poetry – it had that sort of feel to it, the rhythm or whatever – and I thought it was from the Bible. It was at my eye height and carefully copied out – as if the writer was anxious that the message shouldn't be mistaken.

I have to say, I hadn't forgotten about John whilst all this was going on. I just had the leisure, once the vertical hold had been re-established, to look about me and to take in the environment. I didn't think John had belted me over the back of the head, but I didn't remember anything past the gruff voice and the prod of something in the chest.

Eventually, of course, I remembered that I had a bike and that it might be possible to pedal home. It was another ten minutes before I got to my feet, head bent with the lightning of pain that threatened to split my skull, and slowly shuffled through the door to the rear of the hut, to find the path that led to the fence.

Thinking back to that morning, crawling through the hole in the wire was the hard part. Bending down, getting caught on the bare metal and trying to unhook my jacket from its snag tugged at my last reserves of patience.

But my bike was still there, beaded with rain and leaning against the bush. I didn't attempt to ride it until I had gained full control of my legs. I was happy to steer a path between the trees and leave behind the memories of the morning in the camp on the hill.

I was just clear of Wilson's Wood when I saw a police car slowly coming towards me up the track that ran between the avenue of poplars. My mother, Matty and John were in the back.

My mother was first out of the car. She was wearing her fawn three-quarter length coat, so I knew that she had left in a hurry. It was the coat reserved for four star restaurants or a night at the theatre.

'Are you all right?' she asked, holding me by the shoulders and looking into my eyes. 'Where are you hurt?'

'I'm OK, Mum,' I said, embarrassed by all the attention, and also by the presence of John and the law.

'John said you'd fallen and cut your head; that you were unconscious and that he couldn't bring you round.'

'I've got a bit of a headache,' I said, 'but I'm OK, honestly, Mum.'

'Well at least let me have a look at the injury,' she said, parting my hair at the back. 'It's difficult to see much because of the blood, but you've got an enormous bump . . .'

'I think we should just get home,' I said. 'Don't let's bother with casualty, Mum. It's not that terrible.'

The policewoman stepped in at this point. 'I'll just pop your bike in the boot, Graham.' And to Mum, 'I'll drop you off at Wingfield Hospital. He's obviously been unconscious for more than a few seconds so they'll probably want to give him an x-ray to see that he's OK – and to check for concussion.'

So that was that. Police Officer MacAllister was a decent sort. She even got a message through to Dad to explain what had happened. Both the bike and John were offloaded at Sentinel House and we were then taken the ten miles to Wingfield.

Of course when we were alone, stuck in casualty reception, Mum's wrath began to leak out. She wasn't prone to great outbursts of temper, but neither was she the kind of person to bottle up her feelings. 'Your mother is very direct,' Dad had once said, and I think he was referring to the quality of honesty she possessed.

She looked at me carefully with those clear blue eyes: 'I don't know what you were playing at, Graham. That area is out of bounds. There are notices saying "Keep Out" all over the place. The officer said that they have all sorts of unsavoury characters drifting round there – tramps and alcoholics and heaven knows what.'

I sat quietly and let her talk. I think she had probably been frightened by the unexpected change to her plans and she was relieved that I was back in one piece. Matty was definitely happy. She squeezed my arm and told me that she was going to make me a 'get well' card as soon as we got home.

Yet when we got back, and met Dad in the kitchen, he simply skipped the chit-chat: 'I'm glad you're OK Graham but I can't hide my annoyance with what's happened. I had to cancel a meeting with the Publicity Director – who had cancelled a football engagement so that we could talk about the visit from the Douglas-Knight people – and all because you behaved stupidly.

'I've been up to the wood to look around and' – forefinger jabbing – 'I find the area positively spattered with "Keep Out" notices. I don't know if your mother has had a word with you about it, but what would have happened if you'd been knocked out and molested?'

'Brian – Matty's here.'

'Right. I know – but you get my drift.' His voice shifted an octave. He touched my shoulder. 'You're young, I know, but you've got to try and be a bit more – well, you know, responsible.

'And we've also got to be a bit more on the ball about security, Kate,' and he pulled his black case across the table, dark eyes looking up.

'What do you mean?' asked Mum, looking as puzzled as we all felt.

'What I mean,' said Dad, 'is that the sash window to the downstairs' toilet was left unlocked and partly open. The alarm may have been switched on but anyone could have got into the house. And I'm not sure that out here the alarm would have attracted the interest of anyone other than a couple of passing crows.'

'I thought I'd checked everything,' said Mum. 'I know I was in a bit of a flap,' and she pushed aside a lock of hair that hung loose, 'but I'm sure I saw to all the windows – upstairs and down.'

'She *did*,' said Matty, opening a food cupboard.

'Well, it must have come unstuck,' Dad replied and strode off into the study.

'Someone's got a sore head,' I added with as much point as I could muster, pouring myself a glass of water and reaching for the paracetamol from its perch on the microwave.

'Look, he's very preoccupied with this conference,' said Mum. 'I don't know why they've asked him to talk to these people: they've got their own sales staff at Spere. But we'll be entertaining two American gentlemen in a couple of weeks' time. And maybe the MD.'

'What's the MD?' asked Matty, her hand deep in the biscuit tin.

'That's Mr Fletcher. The man—'

'The man who looks like the Fat Controller,' I added, heading for my room.

* * *

I fell asleep during the afternoon. I didn't take up Mum's offer of lunch, and when I woke my mouth tasted of sour milk; there was a pain over the bridge of my nose where my glasses had entrenched themselves and an ache that radiated from the back of my head. Otherwise I felt great.

It was just gone four, the sun tipping its hat in the direction of the west, when the door bell rang.

'Your friend is here,' Mum called up the stairs, and for a moment I wondered who she could mean. It had to be John, of course, but why would he want to come back after the shenanigans of the morning?

'You OK?' he asked when he came into the room.

'Fine,' I said, gesturing towards the chair by the table.

'Nice room you got,' he said, looking about him and ignoring the tea-chest stuffed with junk by the wardrobe; touching the box of games disks by the computer.

'S'OK.'

'Did they give you a lot of grief at the hospital?'

'No. Nothing like that. The pain's eased up.'

'Good,' he said and let the conversation stumble to a halt, its hands in the air.

I flipped on the bedside light.

'What do you think happened, then?' he asked eventually.

'I must have slipped or something when I went into the hut. It wasn't your fault, you know. You gave me a shock and everything by shouting out, but I fell over. I wasn't pushed.'

As I was speaking he turned from inspecting our back

garden and listened with obvious surprise at the narrative. When I finished he startled me by saying: 'I don't follow you.'

'Uh – which part?' I asked. Wondering whether I'd been especially vague in my explanation. To be truthful I felt tired and fed-up and wanted the sickening day to end. The bang on the head hadn't been a great picnic and I resented the telling-off from Dad. And somehow I held John responsible. If he hadn't been messing around, hiding and so on, then none of it would have happened.

'Well, you said something about shouting out? What's that supposed to mean when it's at home?' He flicked through the floppy disks. Tap tap tap.

'Look,' I said, closing my eyes and thinking back over the events. 'I called you and when you didn't answer I figured you were hiding, so I ran to the hut to get out of the rain. Well, you know, as I walked through the door you said something like, "Stop. Who goes there?" and prodded me with a stick or something and the next thing was lights out.'

He looked at me for so long I thought time had stopped.

'That didn't happen,' he said eventually. 'I was poking around amongst a pile of rubbish at the back of one of the huts. Thought I might find a cap badge or belt buckle, you know. I heard you calling, but I didn't come straight away, didn't think there was any rush.'

He stopped for a moment, looking to his right out of the window. 'When I turned the corner of the hut, well, you weren't there. I thought,' and he smiled at the memory, 'I thought you might be playing some kind of trick, you know hiding or something like that, but you weren't.

'I saw your legs as I got level with the doorway. To tell you the truth I thought you were dead. It was really eerie. No one there. The hut empty except for you. I could see the whites of your eyes under your lids. I thought you were kind of looking at me, but then it was obvious you were out cold. I had to bend down and listen to your mouth, to see if you was breathing. But I didn't hit you.'

Nine

Monday morning started in Judaea.

> *'A certain man went down from Jerusalem to Jericho, and fell among thieves, which stripped him of his raiment, and wounded him, and departed, leaving him half dead.*
>
> *'And by chance there came down a certain priest that way: and when he saw him, he passed by on the other side.*
>
> *'And likewise a Levite, when he was at the place, came and looked on him, and passed by on the other side.*
>
> *'But a certain Samaritan, as he journeyed, came where he was: and when he saw him, he had compassion on him.*
>
> *'And went to him, and bound up his wounds, pouring in oil and wine, and set him on his own beast, and brought him to an inn, and took care of him.*
>
> *'And on the morrow when he departed, he took out two pence, and gave them to the host, and said unto him, Take care of him; and whatsoever thou spendest more, when I come again, I will repay thee.'*

'Well students, there you have a story that was told two

thousand years ago in the Middle East. It's about a man who was beaten up and robbed. About people who wouldn't go to his aid, and about one man, who didn't even come from that country, who helped the injured person and took care of him.

'And when it comes to *your* turn, students – and Vincent, I'm looking at you – when it comes to your turn, and your mates say, let's go and take the new boy's bag for a laugh, what will you do?

'Or if you find someone who isn't the most popular person in your class, who needs help, will *you* be the person who provides it, or will you be the one to look away and pretend that nothing has happened?'

I wasn't really giving Mr Parks much attention, I have to admit. Assemblies, particularly on a Monday morning, are times when I find it easier to tune out and think of more pleasant things – the weekend's football or the night's TV. But the Good Samaritan assembly reminded me of Dad in a strange way.

The story seemed to be about mugging someone, and the thought stumbled into my head – for the first time – that it could have been about *Dad*: for what was he other than best mates to a gang of muggers? If you earn your keep helping warplanes to fly then surely – surely? – *your* finger is on the trigger when it's time to start shooting?

After break we had geography with Mr Hardcastle.

'Right, students,' he began, 'quieten down a minute and

I'll tell you what's on the agenda today.'

Like all teachers, he had these little phrases and mannerisms that he tended to use and repeat. He came from the north somewhere, and this too gave an edge to his speech. Lessons always began with him explaining what was 'on the agenda'; we were always 'lads and lasses' and when he had to rebuke some student, the delicious expression used to describe misbehaviour was 'malarky'.

'Right,' he went. 'You'll find you've got an extract from the Craybourne OS map in front of you. Er, you'll find it easier to follow Ramage – Ramage? yes? – if you turn it the right way up. Thank you. OK, as I was saying. On the board there are twenty features that I want you to locate and identify using a six-figure reference. We're all confident about eastings and northings? Sandra?'

'Which comes first, sir, eastings or northings?'

'Er, as you said it, Sandra, eastings first, then northings. Right. You've got twenty minutes for this little exercise. I'll come round and give you a hand should you need my personal assistance – Raymond?'

Quite frankly I always regarded geography as an exercise in common sense. You know: volcanoes bubble up because of magma – a hot porridge-like substance – finding a way to the surface. Rivers flow quickly when there's a steep hill; they tend to slow down when there isn't. The sea usually wears away rock – but you get the picture.

Today there was purpose in looking at the settlements

and the wandering veins of the road system because the map featured Wilson's Wood and the old camp.

I let my eager-beaver classmate, Martin Adamson, work his way through the list ('I think that's an outlier, Graham' – 'Yes, I agree, Martin') whilst I studied the local area. The wood was green and marked with brown contour lines. It was much larger than I had first thought and, as I knew, it surrounded the army camp.

The track from the road was marked as a red dotted line, although the map hadn't included the trees that bordered it. On the far side of the wood was the path of an old railway that had once connected with the main line going to Craybourne. The railway seemed to have come to an end at the wood, or at least the track didn't progress any further.

The shapes of huts in the camp were marked in brown and across the area the words DANGER inserted in red.

'OK,' said Mr Hardcastle, 'we seem to be having a problem locating a dry valley. I don't think you can be looking very hard. There's at least three examples that I know of.'

There was a footpath that left Wilson's Wood in a south-westerly direction, went under a high tension line and then curved back, over the contours to New Barton. The footpath from the old camp came out on the road almost exactly opposite Sentinel House. The camp and the house were linked on the map.

And it occurred to me then, sitting in a classroom at the top of the Humanities block, that I was looking at the route into the past.

I met John at lunchtime. He was with a group of lads on the back tennis court, playing the usual game of fast-forward football.

'You got a sec?' I called as he muscled his way through the defence.

'No,' he yelled when he'd shot wide.

But after an insulting five minutes, he strolled over and leant against the wire, all the time watching the game.

'That head of yours better?' he asked, and then, 'Hey! Scotty, Scotty – come out, get out!' before the keeper was beaten and the ball had bounced off the wire between the two PE bags.

'Fine,' I said. I didn't know where to pick up the conversation. 'What ah – what did you make of the business in the hut?'

'Oh, you mean you thinking that someone was there when there wasn't.' He laughed. 'To tell you the truth, Gray, you had me going there,' he snorted and nudged me in the ribs. 'Made I laugh quite frankly. You was just having us on, weren't you?'

'Well, not really. What I said about the man and everything actually took place.'

'Well then, that bump on the head must have shook up your ideas, you know, knocked your brain box. I'll get it,' he called, and walked out of the court to collect the high-rising ball.

And when he came back: 'Perhaps what happened was that you ran in, slipped on the wet floor and dreamt that someone had a go at you.'

'Look,' I said. 'There's been some odd things happening since we moved in. I thought I'd do some nosing about. Try to get to the bottom of it. You game?'

He ran forward and booted the incoming ball across the tarmac.

'Goal kick,' he yelled against the cries of protest. 'Depends. What'll it involve? Not hours down the library?'

'No, no,' I hurried to reassure him. 'Nothing like that. Just a bit of digging about. That sort of thing. Interested?'

'Maybe,' he replied, stopping to check his watch. 'I'll catch up with you, Gray. It's twenty past. Time for lunch.'

I wandered over to our form room, thinking again about the voice that had rung out the challenge that Saturday at Wilson's Wood. Could it have been someone sleeping rough in the camp? – or was the meeting connected to all the other stuff that had invaded our lives? The stuff that didn't make any sense but which kept leaping out at us, kept wanting to be heard.

When I got off the bus that night, Mum and Matty were waiting at the stop. Before I had a chance to say, 'What are you doing here?' Matty had run up and shouted, 'Look, look what I found Graham,' and she held out a dark object that was hanging from her neck by a piece of string.

I took it in my hands, holding it out under the yellow sodium light so that I could see what she'd got.

'It's a badge,' said Mum. 'She went up the garden as soon as she got home and was busy messing around near the wall. She said you'd be interested. Probably off some soldier's uniform.'

'Do you like it?' asked Matty. 'We can share it.'

Ten

TD/MH: 3.5.99

0001–0048

TD —hello Matty (.) The last time we met (.) a week ago (.) you were telling me about the person you called the ghost (.) in your house (.) do you remember the conversation we had (.)

MH —[inaudible]

TD —you said that the ghost was a man

(2)

TD —you said the man was frightened (.)

MH —bad men wanted to hurt him

(3)

TD —who were the bad men (.)

MH —they had old clothes (.)

TD —what kind of old clothes Matty

(2)

TD —were they wearing – like – rags, clothes with holes in them (.)

MH —they were they were wearing brown clothes (.)

TD —were they wearing the same kind of clothes,

Matty (.) were they in <u>uniform</u> (.)

MH —they were <u>soldiers</u> (.) <u>old</u> soldiers but they weren't old

TD —they were from a long time ago (.)

MH —yes

TD —did they <u>live</u> in your house

(2)

MH —there was a <u>king</u> (.)

TD —a king was on the throne (.)

MH —[inaudible]

(2)

TD —and these soldiers (.) the men in uniform (.) wanted to <u>hurt</u> this man (.)

MH —yes (.)

TD —why was he in danger (.)

MH —he came to my window

(3)

TD —he came to your <u>window</u> (.)

MH —in the <u>night</u> (1) I woke up (.) there was a noise (1) like <u>scratching</u> (2) the light was on outside (.) the light was on so that I could see to go to the window

(3)

TD —did you <u>pull back</u> the curtain

(2)

TD —did you <u>look</u> outside (1)

MH —it was night time (.) I wasn't frightened (.) there was the light and I went over to the window (.) I pulled the curtain (.) I couldn't pull it all the way back because it stuck (.) I saw the room and the door behind me in the glass and then I could see my face looking out and and where my face shone in the glass was the face of this man (.) he was looking at me (.) he was tired (.) his hair was dark (.) it was really wet (.) like he'd been standing outside in the rain (.) he wasn't as old as daddy (.) and I felt so sad that I started to cry (.) not loudly but just like crying and I could see my face in the window and I could see the light and the door behind me but the man wasn't there (.)

Eleven

I was stumbling down a muddy track through a forest of elephant grass. I could feel sweat dribbling down my back and more trickled into my eyes. I could taste salt. Then I entered a clearing, the earth packed hard and brown and dry – like it was used for a meeting place, or something like that.

Mr Parks from school was sitting at a desk in the middle of the open space, writing a letter. He looked up as I came towards him. He smiled and said: 'Take your pick Graham,' and pointed out two paths behind him, each disappearing into the undergrowth. One was signposted: 'Flight' and the other 'Fight.'

And then the door of the bedroom opened and a stranger walked in.

'Right. It's 2.30 in the flipping morning – a Tuesday morning – and I've just had the misfortune to be woken up. And do you know why that is? Have you any idea why I should be wandering round the house at this time of night on the morning when I have to leave the house before six in order to get everything together to participate in the dry-run of next week's conference with the team from Douglas-Knight?'

Dad was standing in the doorway, hands on hips, wearing his red-and-black striped pyjamas. When I'd got my glasses I could see that his hair looked a mess. His face was screwed up like he was in some kind of pain, and the shouting went on. And on.

'I mean, what in heaven's name have you been telling Matty? I mean, what's got into you? Do you do this deliberately? She's five years old for heaven's sake. Five. She's been on the planet sixty-odd months. Now she's seeing faces in the window. I mean. Graham, she's sitting on your mother's knee crying her heart out. Convinced that the dream she'd been having was true.

'I mean, I know that you have talked to your mother about your concern that this property might have the odd ghost in it, but your mother's old enough and sensible enough not to listen to your half-baked ideas.

'Maybe I'm being a bit unsympathetic here, maybe that bang on the head you sustained the other day has affected your judgement.

'But quite frankly Graham, what *really* disappoints me about this episode is that I thought you were too clever for this kind of stupidity. I thought you realised we'd progressed a bit beyond medieval thinking. You know, drawing ludicrous conclusions about things that go bump in the night.

'As far as you're concerned, from now on, the only thing that will go bump in the night is me when I'm mad at you.

'And in future, in future,' (he was stabbing his finger in my direction,) 'don't ever, *ever* talk to Matty about hearing ghosts or seeing ghosts.

'If you still believe this half-arsed nonsense then I'd better make an appointment for you to receive psychiatric help.'

He paused at this point and I knew it was over: he was simply looking for some way to make an exit.

'But no more,' he said finally, holding his hand up. 'I've got enough on my plate without these – interruptions.'

And with that he switched off the light and walked out.

Fear came wide-eyed and cold as soon as he'd finished speaking. I lay there as the dark eased, listening to all the odd noises of the house settling into the night. Waiting for the sound of feet outside, for the door to open and for something to come towards me that was not of our time.

It's easy to smile about it now, but later, when I was in the witness box and struggling with questions, I wondered who else was watching with a sense of impending justice.

I thought about the whole episode during the bus ride into school the next day. John was sitting with his mates at the front so I had the chance to reflect on Matty's experience, Dad's reaction, and the soldier's badge.

It was about the size of a fifty pence coin. Although dark green with dirt, it was possible to make out a crown mounted on a shape that was similar to a Maltese cross.

There was a raised circular plate in the middle that contained some sort of pattern, and the whole design rested on a scroll that probably contained writing.

'Why don't you clean it?' Mum suggested once we'd got back.

'How do you do that?' I asked.

'Yes, Mummy, yes!' said Matty, getting excited.

Mum took the badge, scratching its surface with the sharp point of a curved nail. 'This is probably made from brass,' she said after a while. 'At the moment it's all dark and covered with grime, but if you get some metal cleaner' – and at this point she bent down and rummaged in the cupboard under the sink – 'and let it soak overnight, that might help.'

Before school (and after Dad had long gone) I walked through the wet grass, beyond the apple trees to the brick wall. There was an old compost heap, a galvanised bucket with a hole rusted in its bottom and the ashes of a fire.

Amongst the cinders there was the usual junk you find in such places: bits of broken glass, rusted, half-burnt tins, some unrecognisable pieces of metal. But there was nothing further to connect this place with the army.

I took the badge with me into school.

And had to wait through a morning of Venn diagrams and the problems of the Bennet family in *Pride and Prejudice* before I could get up to the history department.

'Right,' said Mr Pyatt when I discovered him. 'That's a pretty disgusting specimen of a familiar cap badge'.

He was an old man with white hair and strong blue eyes. He had been teaching history since Nelson was a lad and when I introduced myself, I got the impression that my name was of less importance than the contents of the lunchbox he was inspecting.

'You haven't parted with serious money for that heap of junk have you?'

'No,' I replied, irritated by his valuation.

'That's just as well – Graham is it? – because it's not worth anything. They made hundreds of these. Thousands even.'

'Oh,' I said.

'And do you know where you'll find those thousands now? Where the greatest collection of military badges can be located – mmm? eh?'

'I'm not sure,' I said.

'No, I don't suppose you are. Not even an educated guess?' He paused, once again looking up from his desk.

'The Tower of London?'

'Mmm, not bad. Shrewd but entirely incorrect. Look, I'm going to give you a great clue now. The biggest collection of these things can't be found in Britain. They're not in this country at all! So what do you say now Sergeant Cuff?'

Not in this country at all? And there are thousands somewhere else.

'Might the badges be on the remains of soldiers who died in a war?'

His face lit up like a nuclear air-burst. It was as though I'd just beaten the record on a TV quiz show. 'You know, Graham,' he said at last. 'That is an excellent deduction, excellent. And you're not even doing GCSE History – what happened?'

'Geography option.'

'Of course,' he went on. 'Geography option instead. So you give up a subject that would have tested your intellect and you end up spending your time considering the ox-bow lake and the hanging valley. Now, let's get back to business. This piece of metal.

'This is the cross of the Wiltshire Regiment. The scroll at the bottom, if you could clean some of the garbage from it, would say as much. These badges came into use in the 1880s. And they were worn right through both world wars. Take a day trip to Bethune or Bapaume, and dig down a couple of feet in the nearest field, and I bet you'd uncover one of these.'

'So, these were worn by soldiers in the First World War?'

'That's the ticket. Steel helmets didn't come into fashion until the war was eighteen months old and, until then, your Tommy Atkins had little to protect his brains except for the normal regimental hat – with one of these,' he tapped the badge, 'at the front.'

'So, tell me young man,' and again he looked over the top of his specs, 'where'd you get it?'

'My sister found it at the end of our garden.'

'Ah,' and he seemed disappointed. 'Not France then?

Probably discarded by some lad at the end of hostilities. Interesting though.'

And for a moment he turned his attention back to his sandwiches.

'He'd have looked like your man over there.'

And he gestured with his hand towards the long noticeboard.

At the soldier sitting at one of the desks by the window. His hat was pushed back slightly, so that you could see his hair. His face was streaked with dirt and his hands, resting on the table in front of him, were dark with mud and filth. He was unsmiling, grey, still.

Twelve

A trick of the light? An optical illusion? The delayed effects of the bang on the head? I don't know. But for a brief moment, held in the dust floating in that still air, there was a soldier, worn out by the routine of death on the Western Front, seated on the second floor of the Humanities block.

'Mr Pyatt—' I said.

'Ye-es,' and he looked up.

But by then, even as I began to speak, all that remained were the floating motes, the sunlight, and a black-and-white photograph blown up to poster size and pinned to the noticeboard.

'Oh, nothing. I–I just thought I saw something.'

'Ah,' he replied. 'Of course.'

I went over and examined the picture. Close to, a lot of the definition seemed to have washed out and it was less focused. I ran my fingers over the smooth surface.

I turned and saw the teacher staring at me.

'I think I might be suffering from concussion or something. I had a bang on the head a couple of days ago. I,—' I pointed back at the poster, 'thought I saw something over there. Like – I know this sounds daft. It was like the soldier had come to life.'

'Really?' said Pyatt, opening a drawer in his desk.

'I wouldn't give it the time of day, but so much strange stuff has been going on at home.'

There was a long pause. He looked at his watch. He said: 'Like what?'

It took about twenty minutes, I suppose, but I told him everything – about Matty's vision at the window, about the sound of marching in the night, about the incident at Wilson's Wood. He was a good listener, pushing away his lunch-box and allowing me to take up the story from the moment we'd first visited the house. Occasionally he stopped me to check on a detail – 'Matty saw a face?' 'What exactly did you hear in the hut?' – but otherwise he was silent. At the end, when I'd completely finished, he said: 'Did you say you lived at Sentinel House?'

And when I confirmed the fact, he added, 'Most curious, mmm, really,' and he made a note in his diary. It read 'New Barton??'

'Well, there's obviously a lot we don't know,' he said eventually, looking at his watch, 'and we've got barely ten minutes before the bell rings and civilisation rushes to an end. But,' looking straight at me, 'it might be – ah – helpful, if you could find out the history of your house. Who has lived in it; if the local people know anything about it, and so on. But,' and he touched my arm, 'I would be inclined to go easy on your long-suffering parents. If your father has a demanding job, and he's preparing for some big exposition, then I'd try and be a bit – ah – discreet?'

I nodded.

'Good. So, let's see,' and he pulled his blue-covered diary from the pile of exercise books on his desk, 'It's Tuesday now: why not come and see me at about this time – ah – next Tuesday? Should give you time for research and give me time for thought.'

'Oh – and by the way,' he said, as I was just going through the doorway, 'you might like to find out why your home is called Sentinel House.'

Quite frankly it had never really occurred to me. There was the name, chipped out of the stone on our gate posts, carved into the lintel over the front door. There – but strangely invisible.

Sentinel House.

When I look at it now, it seems obvious what its associations are, but then? It was during double science that I borrowed Adamson's dictionary. *Sentinel* nestled between *sentimental* and *sentry*: between the tender and romantic and the watchful and suspicious. A sentinel was a soldier who guarded a military establishment. Someone who was watchful and suspicious rather than tender and romantic.

I thought this over on the bus home. Looking out over the grey December landscape and realising that, for whatever reason, our contact with the military stretched from the past and was now invading our lives.

And as for the figure in the classroom – the worn-out, dirt-covered soldier? He *had* been there, as strongly and as certainly as the tables, chairs, books, chalk dust. He had sat listening and observing and yet had faded as surely as smoke drifting on an autumn afternoon.

It was with this ragbag of thoughts that I crunched up the drive to our house and inserted the key into the lock. As I did this, the front door swung back and I was left looking at the twisted smile of Mr Thomas.

'Oh,' he said immediately. 'I hope I haven't given you another fright. Haven't brought the dog with me this time though, so you're all right. Come in, come in, it is *your* home after all.'

Thirteen

And as he laughed, so one side of his mouth went up and the other came down. I wondered whether he hadn't been involved in some kind of accident, some work-related disaster that had twisted his face like a punched balloon.

'I just called on the off-chance your dad might be in. Hoped to pick that brain of his. Find out how to sort out my modem.'

Mum and Matty came up behind him as I crossed the threshold.

'I can help you with the modem,' I said suddenly. 'If it's just a matter of plugging in, getting the software loaded, that's not a problem.'

'Oh the wonders of youth!' said Mr Thomas, smiling at Mum. 'I was born forty years too early!' And he paused, as though a thought had just struck him. 'I suppose you couldn't show me how you send and receive, using your dad's computer? I mean, I know I might give the impression of being the original thick Taff, but although I feel I can probably get the software side sorted out, I'd quite like a run-through with the application.'

'Suits me,' I said.

'Would that be all right with you, Mrs Hayton?'

'I'll make another cup of tea,' said Mum, already turning and walking down the corridor.

And from Matty: 'You took the badge to school. You did!'

And she stamped off before I had time to explain.

The study is on the ground floor at the front of the house. From the bay window you can look out over the drive to the gate and to the road beyond. Like all the other rooms, it is broad and light with a high ceiling and a fancy plaster rose in the centre.

The farther wall is lined with books, and Dad's table – a treacly brown affair that he'd picked up in some warehouse in Craybourne – faced the door. There is a worn leather sofa and an old armchair.

It was the kind of room that you can imagine would suit a doctor or a lawyer or some other professional person. There was a slight smell of age about the place – a mixture of books and old cigar smoke I suspect.

But the plugboard and tangle of wiring from the monitor and computer spoiled the effect. As did the startling graphic that was framed over the fireplace: the StarRaider.

That day I wasn't entirely comfortable about entering Dad's territory – it wasn't *any* desk after all, with its pots of clips and pens, its pile of paper and box of disks.

I could imagine Dad's disapproval – the raised eyebrows,

dark look. 'What do I need for protection,' he says, 'garlic and a crucifix?'

But I took Dad's place and switched on the power, listening to the whirr of fans and the clicking of the hard disk. Mr Thomas was looking at the files on the bookcase.

'I forgot your dad was in the airplane business,' he said, staring at the StarRaider.

'Well, that's just a part of his work,' I said. 'He's a computer programmer – you know, puts together the code that makes things work in particular ways. You've probably heard about the StarRaider project?'

He nodded, touching the disks on the desk.

The screen came into focus. 'There's the desktop. There's the email application. You double click the icon to load the application. Like so—'

At which point Mum came in and placed two mugs on the table.

'It was three sugars, Mr Thomas?'

'Exactly right, Mrs Hayton.'

There was a kind of oiliness about him that I wasn't comfortable with. Ordinarily I like the music of the Welsh accent, but with Mr Thomas – slippery that's what he was. And sharp too. I got the impression, as he sat next to me and I went through the procedures for sending and receiving, that he knew it all anyway.

I'd just got to the bit where you can hold down Control and Shift in order to monitor the progress of messages, when he gave an exclamation and his mug of tea was rolling away on the carpet.

'I'm *so* sorry, Graham,' he said, standing up. 'I was so taken with your tutorial that I knocked the tea off the table.'

'No worries,' I replied, knowing very well what the incumbent of the room might say. 'At least none of the papers got wet.'

'Or the disks,' said Mr Thomas, looking at the box parked near the screen.

As he didn't make an attempt to go into the kitchen and ask for assistance from Mum, I picked up his mug and said: 'I'll just get a cloth, Mr Thomas, if you'd like to take a seat.'

Although I've never heard Mum badmouth another adult in my presence, I realised by the downturn of her mouth that she was less than enthusiastic about our visitor.

'It might be just as well to keep this to ourselves,' she said. 'Your father's got enough going on to raise his blood pressure without this mishap.' She paused. 'When's he going anyway? He was here an hour before you arrived. Get rid of him, can you?'

I was as good as my word.

I blotted the carpet with kitchen towel and then tapped and clicked through the closing procedures at rather less than novice speed. 'And there you have it, Mr Thomas. You'll be able to send electronic messages right round the world now.'

He stood up, smiling his crooked smile down at me. He

touched my shoulder lightly and said: 'You've been *very* patient, Graham. And I must apologise once again for the mishap with the tea.'

And then nodding towards the StarRaider on the wall, added: 'It's appropriate that the military should be returning to this house. The Winter sisters were a bit of an aberration.'

I followed him to the study door.

'What do you mean?' I asked.

'Well, I don't know all the details, the background and whatnot, but Sentinel House used to belong to the army. Not in my time here, but certainly until after the Second World War. The Winter sisters bought it subsequently. I believe they might well have had some military connection themselves – you know, father in the army, something like that.'

He turned on the doorstep. 'Thank your mother for her patience. If I need further help I'll know where to come.'

Fourteen

Two days later Dad was on the Six O'clock News.

Just after the twenty-minute summary, Helen Draper announced the first successful flight of the StarRaider from a British Aerospace factory in Coventry.

'This is the result of a fifteen-year collaboration between four European partners and promises to provide work well into the twenty-first century,' she said.

There was then footage of the plane making a steep ascent from some anonymous strip and then further glimpses of its slippery form as it made a cautious circuit below the altostratus.

Inevitably, the firm and decisive Defence Secretary talked about how splendid it all was, and then there was Dad, in his navy pin-stripe and red tie, grinning into the camera.

'The key to this aircraft,' he said, in response to a prompt, 'is the onboard computer. Aeroplanes have made use of instruments ever since the Wright Brothers launched their craft in Carolina a century ago, but the StarRaider is different. Take away the computers and the plane simply topples out of the sky: it's inherently unstable.'

'But what's the point of that?' asked the interviewer.

'Well,' and he smiled at the invitation, 'if you want a highly manoeuvrable aircraft, then you need to make it so that it can respond with rapidity to complicated instructions. Human beings do not have the quickness of thought or the deftness of touch to carry out the tasks that are second nature to a computer. This aircraft,' and he gestured to the taxiing form behind him, 'can outfly anything that has two wings and an engine.'

'And so there you have it,' said the correspondent, face to the camera. 'As the century ends we now have an aircraft that can't be flown by human beings. And yet can outsmart all-comers. This is Michael Redfern, BBC News, at Lindon Airfield.'

We were sitting in the lounge – Mum, Matty and myself – and I think we were relieved that everything had gone well. Although the interview was scheduled – the Managing Director of Spere was out of the country and Dad was thought an appropriate choice – there had been panic that morning.

I had been woken by feet thundering up the stairs and Dad shouting: 'Look, Kate,' he said. 'I can't hang around. They were in a buff folder with a red spine.'

'And you left them on your desk?'

'NO. For the last time, I didn't leave them on the table. The folder was resting on top of the computer books immediately behind my chair. I put the stuff together and left them ready last Sunday evening.'

There was the sound of feet going down the stairs and then more voices from the study.

It was the kind of situation to be well apart from. When Dad got into a state he lost the ability to reason: vision and hearing crashed, and concentration – that desktop of calm – became a whirligig of overload.

Yet he was fortunate in having Mum to help him through the crisis, because in situations of this nature she was rarely inclined to panic. She would quietly ask the appropriate questions and then get going on the methodical work of sifting through the evidence. You could tell that she was a policeman's daughter.

All this before six o'clock.

The stuff turned up, although curiously in two locations – the performance specifications were on the bookshelf; the rest of the folder was propped alongside the collection of *Scientific American*.

'Thank God!' I heard Dad say.

'Amen to that,' added Mum. 'And you better get going if you're to pick up Tim Foster en route.'

And that was that. The next time I saw him, he was beaming out of our twenty-one inch, looking for all the world like a calm and capable human being.

They were to use the same footage during the trial.

The following Saturday, which would have been 5th December, I agreed to go into Craybourne with Mum and Matty to pick up a jacket. Although Mum wasn't 'hung up on appearance', as she put it, she felt that denim had too much of the street corner and rather less of the three-course meal about it. And as I was to be present when the Americans pulled in that next Thursday, for the social get-together, something tailored was the order of the day.

Anyway, that Saturday, when I awoke at my usual 7.13, I could tell that there was a thick wadge of snow on the ground: it felt like the house had been wrapped in bandages during the night. When I looked out at the garden, the bushes, lawn, rain-water butt had become vague shapes – as if some busy chef had tripped over a flour sack.

When the phone went at 10.30 I was ambushed by an unexpected voice.

'Ah. Graham,' he said. 'Enjoying the precipitation?' It was Pyatt. 'Look. I won't keep you. Just a lead that you might like to follow up before we meet next week. There's a Miss Violet Thompson in New Barton. An elderly woman who apparently wrote a history of the parish twenty years ago. According to the telephone directory she's at number 6 Underwood Lane. Might be worth talking to. Have a peaceful weekend! Bye.'

And he was gone like a figure in a blizzard.

An hour later and we were in Craybourne: a freezing town filled with pushing, shoving, bad-tempered shapes; stumbling in their bulk through slush; unbalanced by the packed bags they heaved down the wet paths.

But we waited patiently in the red-lighted queue for the

short-stay, and then calmly proceeded to the department stores and the fitting rooms. We were able to maintain this Buddhist detachment because we'd left Dad behind at the keyboard. In fact none of us saw him that morning: just a distant grunt before we left the house. And without his preoccupied self, we were able to carve our path without the need to get it all over quickly – without having to check that the pager was working or to duck into alleyways to call up the answerphone.

And it was also library day, so after we'd sorted the clothes and before we called in for a burger and shake, we dropped our books at the library check-in and agreed to spend twenty minutes looking through the shelves. Or whatever.

There's a couple of computers in the library that people use to access the county database. This is a swanky way of saying you can use the system to see what books were written by particular authors – and whether they happen to be on the shelves of your own library, or somewhere else.

Mr Pyatt had mentioned that a Violet Thompson had produced a history book about New Barton so I carefully tapped in her name and whacked return.

Believe me it's an old system – a CISC 386 I would have thought, so you had to be patient while it did its stuff, the green lettering remaining impassive while the various electrical switches went searching for a match.

And then the main menu disappeared and a text and author frame rolled up.

It hadn't discriminated about Thompson, Violet – the

whole of the Thompson catalogue was thrown on the screen, but there, dead centre, was the entry:

Thompson, Violet, New Barton:
from Domesday to Daleks, 1976

There was only one copy, but the good news was that it could be found in the reference section under Local History.

And yet when I went to look in the appropriate area, there was no such book by Miss Thompson: plenty of stuff about Old Craybourne and local industry; about wildlife and conservation, but no *Domesday to Daleks*.

This was because pamphlets and curious texts not produced by mainstream publishers were locked away in a glass-fronted cabinet. I found this out when I went to ask someone at the desk.

'Well, dear,' she said, a booming Scottish accent breaking the stuffed silence like a brick, 'if you come with me, we'll see if it's been put where it's supposed to be.'

Four minutes later I was sitting with the other researchers, flicking through the eighty-two-page pamphlet in the search for references to the camp at Wilson's Wood and the presence of the military in New Barton. And this is what I found, after chasing the index:

Just after the Boer War, in 1904, the War Office established a small research centre on the hill in what was known as Wilson's Wood.

This is a remote part of the county, two miles beyond

New Barton in the direction of Craybourne. The camp was never to become a site for the employment of local people, as was the case with the larger establishments to the east – at Tydeworth and Bulkington – and rumours proliferated as to what was going on 'up yonder'.

The military maintained a presence up until 1956 when there was an announcement in the local press to the effect that the War Office had deemed the base 'surplus to requirements' and closed it the following year.

Although the government has always refused to explain what use was made of the facility, the elaborate preparations made for withdrawal and closure – which included both the demolition of buildings and the removal of quantities of top soil – suggest that the camp was used for research into, or the manufacture of, noxious substances.

The common belief was that the site was a centre for research into poison gas, and that the railway line that was constructed in 1912 was for the purpose of transporting both raw materials and finished munitions.

And then, two paragraphs further down:

The departure of the army from the camp on the hill coincided with the closure of the Provost Marshal's office at New Barton. Sentinel House had been used as a regional headquarters for the military police since 1908.

At which point I felt a tap on my shoulder. Mum was

standing there, her face pulled into worry.

'Matty's gone,' she said.

Fifteen

I have never met anyone who has died, but at that moment, as Mum stood there surrounded by the orderly shelves of books and the quiet chat of the reference section, I felt our world tumbling apart and the space that had been filled with chatty, excited Matty was now being covered with a scattering of gravel and earth.

'Where—'

'I've looked all round the library,' she said. 'C'mon, you'll have to help me. She's not here Graham.'

The thing was, in those few moments, I couldn't even remember what clothes she was wearing. Whether she'd travelled out in her cagoule and striped bobble-hat; whether she had on her red coat. And blue scarf? Skirt and tights – or jeans?

But I followed Mum, who was in danger of running out of control. She seemed to be having difficulty controlling her breathing, and she hadn't waited to explain what we were supposed to do. I wondered whether Matty wasn't tucked away somewhere reading a book or was looking at the pictures painted by the children from a local primary school which dominated the far wall.

When I caught up, I tugged her arm, managed to ask; 'Mum, wait: what was she wearing. Was it—'

'The – her red dress – coat! Look, this, this is – impossible!'

And I thought that she was going to cry, turning away and heading for the checkout.

But no one in the reception area had seen a little girl with blonde hair and a red coat. And yes it was possible that she could have slipped through the barrier, although if she'd tried to take a library book out the alarm would have registered. And yes they would be happy to look out for her if we'd like to search outside.

Which was almost the end, because once through the swing doors, we were immediately confronted by a great Amazonian flood of people, all dark clothes and exhaled breath; pushing and shoving their way towards the covered market.

'Look, Mum,' I said, once more touching the sleeve of her coat. 'Stay here. Don't move from here. Matty might be still in the library. And if she's slipped out, she might be trying to find her way back. You keep a watch for her. Stay here for a minute or two. I'll look in the gardens by the Art Gallery.'

She nodded, completely defeated by the situation and as convinced as I that Matty had either wandered off or had been taken away by some sinister stranger.

I went down the steep flight of steps, and turned into

the crowd, away from the town centre. It was like trying to swim against a strong current, my progress hindered by obstacles that might just as well have been fallen trunks – prams, pushchairs, double-buggies, shopping trollies, bags stuffed with purchases.

But eventually, I made the two hundred metres, beyond the Victorian front of the town art gallery, and went up the stairs between the iron railings and into the library gardens.

'Hello,' she said, almost straight away. 'I thought you would find me.'

She was standing on a stone shelf before the Roll of Honour to the Glorious Dead of the 1914–18 war. It was the list that named those killed in action.

'Oh Matty!' I said, running to her, 'we've been so worried. We didn't know where you'd got to.'

'I'm sorry,' she said. 'I only just got here Graham. I've found the *name*, Graham. The man in our house – is a soldier – there—'

And with that, her small hand reached up and touched a space after the name 'Weston'.

I followed her pointing finger, examined the grey stone of that frozen parade. But there was no name there, not even a pattern thrown by the light.

'What, Matty?' I said. 'What do you mean?'

Again she touched the place and half-turning said, 'It's what he *said* – "Whitaker, Paul Edward". Can you see now?'

But that name wasn't there, it wasn't listed with the Harrisons and Joneses and Wainwrights and Carters. Yet she'd obviously heard something because where else did Whitaker, Paul Edward come from?

'Look, Matty. We've got to tell Mum. We've got to get back to the library. She's almost out of her mind with worry. Because she – we thought – someone had taken you – someone bad.'

I'm not going to detail Mum's reaction. But even after everything – even after what was about to happen, she never forgot this as being one of the worst moments of her life. Almost as though she had been physically harmed in some way.

The burger bar was quite a strained affair. I think Matty felt guilty, but also excited. She was sad that she had wandered off without giving notice, but pleased to have discovered the identity of our visitor.

I wanted the time and the place to talk to her about it, to discover what compulsion had made her leave the library and get to the war memorial, because the other strange thing about it was that although five and a half at that time, Matty couldn't read. Yet the place where Whitaker might have appeared in the list of dead men was the place where her finger had touched the stone.

Once clear of Craybourne, the journey back to New Barton was straightforward. Mum didn't break the speed limit, but until the turning from the main road, we were able to travel on a surface that glistened darkly in the late afternoon sun.

As we drove along the lane, John Franklin slipped off the wall that bordered our house. He shielded his eyes against the glare of our headlights, and then pulled open the gates, following us whistling a particularly off-note tune.

'He sounds happy,' said Mum.

'Thought you might want to come out,' he said when I emerged from the back. 'Go for a ride or something?'

'We've been into Craybourne,' I said.

'I called earlier but there was no one at home. Thought I'd wait and see.'

'Look, John, there's a couple of things I've got to do this afternoon, but I don't think I'm doing anything tomorrow. Maybe the afternoon?'

'You're looking after Matty in the afternoon, Graham,' said Mum, turning the key in the boot. 'We've got to be at Tim Foster's at two-thirty so I was banking on you as babysitter.'

'Look, what about the morning?'

'Yes,' he said. 'About ten then. We'll do something.'

And he left us to get the shopping out of the car.

Dad had been picked up by a friend to have a look at garden ponds, so there was no one home when we got inside. Dark and silent, as ever. Just the usual groans of the ancient pipework when I ran the water for the kettle and when Mum flipped the switch on the central heating.

We were in the kitchen when I heard footsteps hurrying over the gravel.

'He's back early,' said Mum, looking at her watch. 'I wasn't expecting him before five.'

But the footsteps seemed to recede. Once heard, the crunch of gravel softened, so that whoever had been in the yard must have been moving away from the house.

I went down the corridor and opened the front door to check, but apart from the gate being slightly ajar, there was no sign of any secret lurker. The road was deserted and the street light glowed orange.

'Don't tell,' said Mum, holding up Matty's new dress, 'your famous ghost has been paying us a daylight visit?'

'No,' I said. 'There was no one there, Mum. Perhaps we were simply imagining footsteps. Or was it that aural mirage thingy that Dad was talking about?'

I'm not usually sarcastic, but I felt she was talking about something she didn't understand, had no knowledge of. I hadn't told her what Matty had been up to in the Library Gardens, and I was also convinced that whoever had been walking across our yard hadn't been the spirit of Paul Edward Whitaker.

But we made our peace. We were both shocked by the nightmare absence of Matty, and I think she was grateful that I'd been there to steer a path through the threatening chaos of those moments.

At just gone four I found Violet Thompson's name in the phone book. In Underwood Lane as Mr Pyatt had said.

After two attempts at the number, a strange, withered voice came on the line: 'Hello. This is New Barton 781542.'

'Hello,' I said, totally unrehearsed. 'Is that Miss Thompson?'

'It is. Who is it calling, please?'

'My name's Graham Hayton, Miss Thompson. I live just down the road from you in New Barton and I'm doing some research on the village – well, and the area round about.'

'I see.'

'I know that some years ago you wrote a pamphlet on New Barton—'

'Over twenty years ago. I'm sure that it's all pretty much out of date now.'

'Well, what I was wondering, Miss Thompson, was whether I could pay you a visit over the next couple of days to ask you a few questions about the area?'

'I'm not sure I can be of much use to you – did you say your name was Graham? Well, I did all the research in the early seventies. I've still got my files and everything, my research papers, but I haven't looked at them for years. I was hoping that some publisher might be interested in my work and offer to pay the costs of printing and distribution and so forth, but no such luck, I'm afraid.'

And she laughed at herself, her voice echoing round what I imagined to be a dark and empty hallway.

'But there's a copy of my pamphlet in the library at Craybourne and they've probably got a lot more recent research since I was writing. Oral history has taken off lately, you know.'

'I appreciate that, Miss Thompson, and I've seen your pamphlet in the library, but the thing is I've – or rather my family – has recently moved into Sentinel House and it was about the house that I wanted to question you.'

There was silence – so long that to begin with I thought I must have said something offensive. And then wondered whether she'd accidentally caught the cradle and cut us off.

'Miss Thompson—'

'I'm still here,' she said. 'You've moved into Sentinel House, you say?'

'That's right.'

'Well then, I think there's nothing for it. You'll have to come round and we'll have a chat. I'm assuming you know nothing about it?'

'Only what you wrote in your pamphlet.'

'Right. Then there's something you *should* know. Could you call in – let me see – tomorrow I've got the ladies from the WI in the afternoon and next week's not at all convenient, but you might like – are you at school Graham? Forgive me for asking, but your voice sounds quite young.'

'Yes,' I replied. 'I'm fifteen. I go to James Gray Comprehensive.'

'I see. Would you like to come to tea next Friday? At about five o'clock?'

The bus usually got me back by 4.30 and there was nothing planned in the house that I knew of. The Americans were due on the Thursday – the 10th – so

Friday sounded all set and raring to go.

'That would be very good,' I said.

'And do you eat seed cake Graham?'

'I think so.'

'Then I'll make one especially. It was Paul Whitaker's favourite.'

Sixteen

And she put the phone down.

It was like watching one of those old TV programmes where something terrible or amazing threatens and the picture freezes and a voice says: 'Tune in again for the next exciting adventure of—'

And you're left spending the following day on the bus and during registration trying to figure out how the characters are going to escape from some situation or wondering whether or not some person actually *did* commit the crime.

The creepy thing about this call was that no sooner had Matty, with all the seriousness of a five-year-old, established the identity of our visitor, than Miss Thompson, with whom I had never so much as exchanged a 'good morning', had as near as dammit validated our experience.

Tea in the kitchen was a fragmentary affair. Matty was happy to chat about the video she'd just been watching where one of the presenters was being made up as a pantomime dame. Mum listened politely and asked occasional questions, and Dad, head down with preoccupation, shovelled spaghetti and sauce into his mouth with all the relish of a machine.

I caught up with Dad just before the mid-evening news. He was in the study and, as he'd left the door slightly ajar, I wandered in.

He was flicking through pictures from a book about low-maintenance gardens: you know, 1001 uses for concrete and paving slabs.

'Dad,' I began, as he still hadn't looked up. 'What do you know about poison gas?'

He placed a hand on the page, looked up and said, 'You mean as a weapon of war? That kind of thing?'

He had changed from his working clothes – white shirt, jacket and tie – and I recall he looked younger, less threatening in jeans and sweatshirt.

'Yes – that kind of thing.'

'I'm not an expert, Graham,' lines of concentration forming trenches on his forehead, 'but phosgene and chlorine – gases used in the First World War – were by-products of the chemical industry. I think' – and he looked to his right at the lines of books on his shelves. 'No, we used to have a paperback on the war that would have told you about gas attacks. I'm under the impression that they weren't brilliantly successful at the time.'

'They killed people though?'

The silence turned the room into a cavern.

He seemed to examine my face with the scrutiny you'd

normally expect if you went to the doctors complaining of terminal acne.

'Look,' he said, 'why don't you see if there's anything on the Mitchell-Davies CD-ROM? I'm going to be using the PC this evening, but go ahead – in the morning – that's if you still need to know about these – er – weapons of war.'

Was that sarcasm? Or irony? Did he place the stress on 'weapons' – or not? Who am I kidding, anyway?

John turned up at just gone nine the next morning, characteristically going round the side of the house and whacking the back door with such ferocity that Mum snatched it open and said, 'We're not dead you know.'

He looked up at her, startled for a second, before recovering himself with: 'I'm sorry Mrs Hayton. I didn't know you'd be up at this time. Thought I'd give her a belt just in case you were upstairs.'

'Right. Well,' she said. 'You'd better come in. Graham is just finishing his breakfast.'

'Right you are then,' he said without embarrassment. 'OK Graham?'

He sat down, and turned to the back of the paper. 'See that Swansea have got a new manager, then.'

'Oh? That's fascinating.' I spooned more cereal. 'I need to check a couple of things on the computer. Before we go. OK?'

'And I could have a shot at one of the games you've got stacked?'

'Later. This will only take a sec.' I dumped the bowl. Led the way into the study.

The Mitchell-Davies CD-ROM is one of those encyclopaedias that come 'bundled' with PCs. It's not the most comprehensive research tool and the index is off-whack. Look up 'gas' and you'll find everything about domestic consumption but nothing about the stuff used to slaughter people. For that you needed to check 'chemical warfare'.

John wasn't exactly in love with the investigation, and after a while he went to look out of the window.

Dad wasn't far off in his identification of the gases used in the First World War. The pattern was that one side would fire gas shells or release the substances from storage tanks against the enemy in nearby trenches, and then the other side would do the same.

I scrolled on down.

At the top of the page titled *Gas Attacks in the First World War* there is a black-and-white photograph of soldiers in a line. Each man is holding on to the shoulders of the person in front. You can tell it's winter because they're wearing heavy coats. Each person has his eyes covered with a thick, white bandage.

One young man, wearing a sergeant's stripes, holds his face with his left hand.

The slight blur of movement at the foot of the picture tells you the photographer has caught these men on the move; in your head you can hear the slow shuffle of their feet as they trudge out of the frame to some unknown destination.

The picture is simply titled, *Gas Victims, Ypres, 1917*.

Looking back, I think I'd got this idea that people who were gassed died pretty quickly, like it was a quick gasp of poisoned air and the victim fell dead. Or if they didn't die, they'd spend a few days in hospital and be all right. Perhaps with a cough or something.

But it wasn't like that. There were plenty of facts about chlorine and phosgene, but the section on mustard gas kept me fixed to the screen.

Mustard gas created great blisters on the skin, in the mouth and nose; in the windpipe and down into the lungs. It glued eyes shut with a sticky mucus, caused violent vomiting – and killed. Men were strapped to their beds because of the pain, their cries reduced to hoarse whispers as they struggled – choked – for breath.

And they died blind and alone.

It must have been the silence of the keyboard that alerted John to the fact that I'd finished and was simply sitting in Dad's chair.

'Can we go yet?' he said.

And I can remember looking up at him as though from another world and simply saying: 'Yes.'

Later, as we cycled past the Alms Houses by the stream in the village, where Underwood Lane joins Craybourne

Road, John shouted across; 'I live down there,' pointing to a row of red brick council houses. 'The one that's got the Ford outside – the white one.'

'Oh, right,' I said.

He stopped at the junction. 'My Dad has just started his own business.' He laughed. 'Not exactly a multinational. He's using our shed as a sort of workshop. To make things.'

'Make things?'

'Yes. He's good with his hands, you know. Got a lathe and all sorts in the shed. Makes rocking-horses for a company in London. He can make one a week.'

We sat on our saddles and looked up the road. I couldn't see number six, where Miss Thompson lived, but I had a picture of John's Dad, some huge craftsman working on his rocking-horses in a shed filled with wood and machinery and the smell of sawdust.

'Do you know Miss Thompson?' I asked John.

'Miss Thompson?'

'Lives at number 6.'

'White-haired old biddy? Sometimes walks with a Zimmer?'

'Dunno. Never seen her, but I know she lives round here.'

'Yeah,' he said at last. 'That's the one. Ancient. Can hardly walk. Really stooped. You know. Bent over,' and he gave an impression of the angle of stoop that Miss Thompson possessed. 'You'd think she was carrying cement on her back.'

We spent the rest of the morning on the treed ridge

above the farm. The bridle path wound along the top for about half a mile before dropping down the slope into a tussocky, overgrown field that led to the road.

Where the snow had melted, the path was puddled and muddy; elsewhere just so much slush. As we hurtled along the ridge, the trees on either side breaking up the landscape like a moving picture reel, I wondered for the hundredth time about the way all the clues seemed to be joining together faster and faster – like Matty and the plaque to the Glorious Dead and then my conversation with Miss Thompson.

I caught up with John just before the ridge gave out. He was half-turned towards me, beside the great trunk of an upturned tree.

'Toppled over one night in February,' he said. 'One hell of a gale. Stripped tiles off some of the houses in the village and turned this old feller on its head.'

We rested our bikes on the ground and spent some minutes climbing along the bough, now horizontal, to the point where it tipped over the edge of the slope and hung out six or eight metres in the air.

'John,' I said. 'Why do you always come round the side of the house? Most people go to the front door.'

It was a question that I'd wondered about before but had never remembered to ask. Anyone can walk up to the front of a house, but to go through the gate and round the side is sort of invasive. Like burglary.

'Habit,' he said, walking out over the drop. He turned

slowly, and then jumped. The tree quivered but didn't move. 'Yeah, habit,' he said, looking down. 'From when we worked on the house for the Winter sisters. We always used the side entrance.'

He pulled at an old twig attached to a branch.

'They were OK but I guess they thought tradespeople should go round the side. You know, only the gentry were allowed in through the door at the front.'

'So they were—'

'Stuck up?' and he pushed the tip of his nose with a forefinger. 'Probably. I just remember them as a couple of old biddies. Liked to talk. Moved like ghosts. You could be painting a skirting board and turn round to refresh your brush and one of them would be standing over you, watching your every move. Bit creepy if you ask me.'

'Right,' I said, filing away this latest bit of information about Sentinel House and its past. More disconnected fragments.

Instead of retracing our path, we took the steep slope down into the abandoned field, hurtling through the old snow and mud, splashing through concealed pools and skidding on ice. We fetched up by a stile that was partly hidden by the surrounding hawthorn.

Later, as we approached Underwood Lane, John said, 'Come and have a look at the workshop. The old man's just finished one of the horses. Hasn't started to paint it yet. You'll be amazed.' And again, he laughed.

The house was on the corner, on the right. The G-reg

Ford was still there. The tax disc had run out. We went through the metal gate and up the concrete path to the right of the lawn.

'Here,' he said, 'lean your bike against the fence. It'll be all right. Not many thieves round here.'

The shed was a breeze-block building at the back, running the full width of the garden. The long window was screened with a Venetian blind, and as we approached I could hear someone whistling.

There was something familiar about it all that I wasn't able to put my finger on then, but when John opened the door and I'd absorbed the single bulb, the unpainted rocking-horse and the rack of tools, I was face to face with the twisted smile of Mr David Thomas.

'Hi,' said John. 'This is Graham.'

Seventeen

TD/MH: 17.5.99

0001–0010

MH —We went down (1) We were (.) alone (.) Locked in (1) It was dark (.) There was a window (.) It was grey (.) There were cobwebs (.) I thought of spiders crawling (1) In the dark (.) We could (.) We could hear people's feet above (.) In the room above (.) There were other sounds (.) We listened

(3)

—When when we opened the window (.) It didn't want (.) It was hard to open the window (.) We couldn't get out (.) There were bars (.) There was no other way (.) We were left (.) In the dark with loud footsteps.

Eighteen

'Ah, Graham,' he said, wiping his hands on his apron. 'Good to see you. Been out for a ride, I understand?'

I wasn't in good shape for a chat so I could hardly stumble out anything sensible. I nodded in an idiot kind of way.

'Bit of a surprise, is it?' He went on, John going over to the bench at the far side to pick up a chisel.

'I'm John's stepdad you see. I've been with his mam for so long that we're like one cuddly family these days. We all live together, work together and' – he laughed – 'play together.'

He smiled and the strings on his face clenched into a kind of grimace.

'You'll be pleased to understand that I've got the old modem up and running. Goes like a rocket now. Next step: the internet! But enough of that, what do you think of my new-found hobby? If you were a bit smaller I'd let this little fellow take you for a ride,' and he patted the wooden flank of the horse. It moved backwards under his touch as if slowly coming to life.

'Course I'd be nothing without my trusty helper and his

spray gun,' and he gestured towards John who was tapping his chisel into a block of wood clenched in a vice.

'I didn't know you ran your own business,' I was able to say at last, whilst looking round through the particles of wood dust at the discarded tools on the bench, the set of goggles and face masks on the wall, the tattered seaside calendar and the picture of some guy with a beard, black hair and stubby cigar.

'Well, bit early to say "business" yet,' he said. 'But we live and hope. And if you'll now excuse me – John – I need to get this chap on his way before five this afternoon.' He pulled his face mask down and reached for the electric sander.

Outside there was a slight gauze of rain in the air and the sky was layers of grey, like discoloured ice-cream.

'You never told me he was your father,' I said. 'He's been in our house, you know.'

'I know,' said John. 'I couldn't see the point. And it was sort of' – and he paused to get the words right – 'awkward. You know – saying he's my dad, but he's not my dad and we have different names and everything. I mean, does it matter?'

I thought about this as my bike ticked slowly down Underwood Lane and past the silent number 6. It was all so strange. Spending time with John and helping his stepdad – but neither of them acknowledging the existence of the other.

I explained my discovery to Mum on my return. She

was in a kitchen soft with steam and warmth, carefully paring a bowl of brussels sprouts. All she could say, having turned off the radio, was, 'I expect he was a bit embarrassed. You know. Mr Thomas and John's mum might simply be living together. And there's all that business of different names to explain away. No,' she said finally. 'I don't really find it that odd. You know,' and she turned towards me smiling in a knowing kind of way, 'people get worried about all sorts of silly things.'

Well, quite frankly I couldn't see what she was getting at, so after checking another dismal Chelsea report in the paper, joined Dad in the study.

I can't really say why I needed more discussion with the resident war-monger, particularly as he was nine parts preoccupied with selling his deadly know-how to the Americans, but I think I wanted in some way to discuss with him what I'd found on the CD-ROM. It seemed that the use of gas was almost playground stuff: first one side would attack the opposition – killing thousands – and then the other side would do the same. Wasn't this really all there was to it? Grown men with dangerous toys.

And I think also, and maybe I write this because of what has happened, there was somewhere knocking around my idea of the 'old dad'. He wasn't ever like the father in that Roald Dahl movie – *Danny, Champion of the World* – but before he became a creature of Spere Electronics, and when I was small, he seemed to have more time.

He and Mum had this agreement that he would read the

bedtime story twice a week. And at first he would turn up in my bedroom in the old house and pick up whatever was current on the pile of books and would do his best to inject life into the reading.

But I don't think his heart was ever in the project: I think fiction, even the picture-book variety, bored him stupid, so that one evening, when the light was fading and my bedside lamp glowed orange, he came in and sat on the bed and said something like: 'Would you like me to tell you a story tonight? Not from a book or anything, but just like – ah – talking to you?'

And I said something like: 'What would the story be about?'

And he said: 'About an amazing man who changed the world.'

And I said: 'Let's go!'

And that's when Isambard Kingdom Brunel entered my life. Quite frankly, with a name like that and the way Dad told the story over the next few weeks, I thought he was making it all up and that Brunel was more or less a figure like the Big Friendly Giant, particularly because he was engaged in such amazing stuff – getting washed out of tunnels under a river; inventing an amazing new form of transportation; throwing a bridge over a two hundred–foot gorge, but when we all went to Bristol, and we saw the slender beauty of the Clifton bridge, with Brunel's name engraved on the uprights, it was like finding out that there was a Father Christmas.

There is even a picture of Brunel in Dad's study, on the notice-board behind his desk: a small man in a top hat, chewing on a cigar, and completely overshadowed by this huge pile of massive chains that were being used to launch Brunel's ship, the *Great Eastern*.

Anyway, this gives you a bit of the context as I wandered down the corridor that morning to chat to Dad. I stuck my head round the door, trying to switch on my Mr Affable expression, but he didn't even look up from the monitor.

'I'm a bit busy at the moment. I should be done soon.'

I'd like to write here that I went down later and we had a good old chin-wag, father and son. But this isn't a cosy soap opera. And no, it didn't happen.

Nineteen

Mum and Dad were going over to visit their friends that afternoon. The Fosters lived on the other side of Craybourne, and Mum and Dad were due at 2.30, so they were ready and by the front door a little after ten to.

'Right,' said Mum. 'The number is by the phone if you need to call. There are biscuits in the cupboard and some banana cake in the tin. We'll be back by—' she looked at Dad who was standing with his hands stuffed into his overcoat pockets.

'Six?' he suggested.

'We'll be back between six and half past. OK?'

And they went out, through the door and into the overcast yard. It was 6th December.

Matty and myself hadn't spent much time together, so it was slightly odd, just the two of us in that large house. She didn't seem concerned that Mum and Dad had gone out and we both got set in front of the TV. This wasn't my number one Sunday pursuit, but I thought it would be a friendly thing to do.

There wasn't a terrific choice, when it came down to it, and after watching a sequence called *Cartoon Cavalcade*, we tuned into a film and fetched up on some palm-fringed coast watching eighteenth century pirates make their way across a pile of rocks. They were following a map that one of them was clutching, and eventually they discovered the mouth of a sea-cave. This was where the buried treasure was supposed to be. Well, after about five seconds of watching them shift sand, Matty tugged at my sleeve.

'Graham,' she said, 'have you been in the cellar?'

'Yeah – once in a while. It's not very interesting you know. Just old boxes and Dad's collection of bottles.'

'Well, could we have a look in a minute?'

I couldn't really see the attraction, quite frankly, but if that was her heart's desire, let's do it, I thought.

'Sure,' and I got up. 'We'll have a look now.'

I should explain that the cellar extends for about half the floor area of the house. The entrance is via a door in the panelled wall under the stairs.

The room isn't enormous, or anything, but is slightly creepy because the light switch is concealed on one of the beams that supports the ground floor. And unless you take some light with you, you're wandering in the dark.

That day I didn't know where a spare torch was, but I recalled the basement window gave some light, and so we went down the steps, turned to the right under the old gas pipework and found ourselves in a space filled with shadows, old boxes and the dark stain of damp that spread across the floor and up the wall.

'It smells funny,' said Matty, holding my hand.

'Yeah – it's just the damp. These bricks' – and I pointed – 'rest on the earth. Now let me just see—' and I started to feel the sides of the overhead timbers for the hidden switch.

'Ssshhh!' she said suddenly, clutching my pullover. 'What was that noise?'

Neither of us moved. Her fear seemed to infect the room and I felt the hair bristle on the back of my neck.

At first, in the twilight, I couldn't make anything out. The house seemed unusually silent, but then, quite clearly and quite distinctly, came the first footfall of someone walking above. They weren't making a lot of noise, but the clear tap of a tread on the kitchen tiles came down to us.

Matty seemed to be shivering, leaning against me for comfort. Neither of us spoke. Both of us knew that the cellar door was pulled back and completely visible to anyone walking through the house.

And then the sound stopped, as if someone was up there listening – like one of those house spiders you sometimes see in the evening, halfway out of the dark, front leg poised, waiting. That silence, as we strained to hear, was almost worse than the first tread and it got to the point when I thought we'd imagined something, that it was really just the house giving one of its periodic groans. But we hadn't, because the slow touch of a stranger crossing the floor came down to us, and the footsteps didn't stop.

Tap tap tap, slowly and steadily, travelling to where we stood.

I think it was more an instinct for survival that made us move towards the wall and away from the centre of the room at the precise moment a long shadow began to flow down the stairs, dripping step by step until we knew that the intruder was standing at the opening, looking down.

The figure waited and waited. Listening.

I don't think breath passed my lips in thirty seconds. The world seemed to have shrunk to a fifteen-year-old boy and a terrified child trying to conceal themselves in the half-dark.

And then – well – the black stain abruptly flowed back up the stairs and the cellar door banged shut. The key turned and we were locked in.

At that point, her body shaken by a series of great shudders, Matty started to cry. Not loudly, but like a car starting on a cold day, a few great heaves of effort, and then the tears fell with the sudden release of tension. I hunkered down beside her; I whispered, 'It's OK Matty. We're all right.'

All the time listening for sounds up above.

I think she was too wise to the situation to completely give in to her feelings, and I think she also realised that whoever had entered our house might also return to the cellar; might also come down that flight of steps and find us there.

And so we stood and listened, trying to make out the tremor of human activity in the rooms above.

The person was in the study.

There was absolutely no doubt about the fact. Over to the right, I heard the electronic spring of the monitor being turned on and then the squeak of someone sitting down at the swivel chair.

I put my finger to my lips and crossed the room to the window. It was filthy with dust and cobwebs and neglect. The frame was beginning to rot and the fastener in the middle difficult to turn. And yet when I did ease back the clasp, the window seemed cemented together, locked as if both edges had been liberally pasted with glue.

I paused, and looked up at the sky glimpsed through the metal grid that shut us off from the outside world and then turned to Matty and shook my head. There was no point in opening the window if we couldn't get through the bars to the garden above.

We listened to the house for a few moments, but it was completely silent. No sound from the study. No footsteps. I waited for a minute longer and then went over to the steps, carefully treading through the minefield of old boxes.

You could see a strip of light from the hall shining in at the foot of the door, but once at the top, the handle firmly grasped, it was obvious we weren't going to escape that way.

Matty hadn't moved when I got back; standing still in the middle of the cellar and looking up at the ceiling.

It was at this moment that I saw the white plastic of the switch. There didn't seem to be any point in not giving ourselves some light, particularly as the intruder must know that we were there.

And yet when, moments later, the area was flooded by the single bulb, I think we both felt horribly exposed. The shadows gave the illusion of security, but now there was no place to run.

'I don't like this,' said Matty. 'They might see us. It's too much light.'

And I gave in to her feelings, partly, I must admit, on account of my own uneasiness at our situation. And so, for twenty minutes, we sat in semi-darkness on wooden boxes and waited for the intruder to go.

Eventually, of course, they did.

Matty and myself both looked up at the same time when we heard the snap of a wall socket being switched. And then the muffled sound of feet over the carpet. To the door, then down the corridor, almost directly overhead, to the cellar entrance.

For one brief moment, they stopped there, waiting not fifteen metres from where we sat, and then moved on, through the kitchen. Then silence. No sound of a gravel tread. They must have disappeared over the back wall into the cow field.

I pressed the light switch.

'Are you all right?' I said.

'Yes, I think so,' she replied, her face smudged with dirt.

'I think we'll be safe now. Although it might get a bit chilly waiting for Mum and Dad.'

Two minutes later, Matty got up from her box and went over to the wall next to the old coal chute. She brushed away some dirt and then turned and said. 'Come and see, Graham. Look.'

And there, quite faint but cut into the dark brick were the letters: PEW.

I stared at them for a moment, seeing only the uneven spacing and shape of the lines. Then something nudged my memory: 'Paul Edward Whitaker,' I said.

Twenty

The marks were low-down, about ten centimetres from the ground. And after the 'W' could be made out one of those government arrows that prisoners once wore on their uniforms in old times.

'The arrow points down,' said Matty, outlining the mark with her forefinger. 'Perhaps there's something buried there.'

And I had a flash of the TV pirates shovelling Hollywood sand to reach their treasure chest.

'No, no, Matty. That's a mark that indicates the property of the government. They used to stamp all sorts of stuff with it, including the clothes worn by convicts. I think it shows that PEW was a prisoner here.'

'And that was why he was sad?'

'I expect so,' I replied and I went back to my box.

She wandered round the room for several minutes, occasionally touching the walls and sometimes bending down to peer into the dark of the corners.

'Do you think we could lift some of the bricks – over there – where the arrow points?' she said after completing several circuits. 'Please.'

The floor of the cellar was completely bricked over and as far as I could see the builders hadn't used any mortar. That explained the damp of the area and it probably wouldn't be too hard to move a brick or two if you were enthusiastic about seeing what was underneath.

The problem was, they were tightly packed together and to lift one would require an implement the width of a knife to slide down between the two surfaces and exert some force.

I explained this to Matty and the pair of us looked through the boxes scattered across the floor in the hope that an abandoned picnic hamper, packed with cutlery, might materialise.

It was whilst we were rifling through bottles and jam jars, and all the other dusty paraphernalia that the phone began to ring upstairs in the hall.

We both stopped and waited. It went on and on and on. And then stopped.

'Probably someone for Dad,' I said. He received most of the telecommunications traffic in the house. But then the ringing started again. And as before continued for the best part of two minutes. There was an urgency about the call, as if they expected someone to lift the receiver and were just checking in case they'd mis-dialled.

'It could be Mummy,' said Matty. 'Phoning to see that we're OK.'

'Yeah,' I said. 'And if it is them, they'll call again. I bet you.'

It had turned four and already the sky outside, through the window, was three-quarters night, and this made the room darker. The light was no better than 60 watts, and threw great shadows across the floor and walls.

'What about this?' said Matty suddenly.

It was an old steel ruler. I thought it was a fraction too thick but we had nothing better to work with, so I said, 'OK. Let's give it a go.'

Trying to slide that piece of metal between bricks that had been jammed together for decades was difficult, and it took me several frustrating attempts before I realised that I might have better luck should I push the ruler down the side which had contact with the wall.

Five minutes of this and I went back and sat on the box.

'I think we're getting somewhere Matty, but this could be a long job.' At which point, the phone in the hall started to give out its call sign.

'What did I tell you?' I said. 'They'll realise something's wrong and they'll be on their way.'

Or so we hoped.

The major breakthrough came when Matty saw movement as I exerted maximum pressure and, eventually, we were able to insert the metal along one of the ends. This opened up a crack about a tenth of a millimetre.

When we finally lifted the brick clear we both bent over the dark gap to see if our treasure was waiting collection. But there was only densely packed earth marked with the imprint of the Portsmouth Brick Company.

After all that work – it was gone 4.30 by this time – all we had retrieved was a lump of baked clay.

Matty touched the cold surface of the earth with her fingers, and then delicately, slowly, scraped away a centimetre to uncover the shape of a heavily rusted tin box, two-thirds the length of the brick we had just removed.

She looked up at me.

'I was right, wasn't I?' she said, her mouth spreading into a jaw-breaking grin. 'We have discovered treasure.'

Twenty-one

I took out another brick to give us room for manoeuvre, and then, very carefully, sensitive to its age, brought out the box.

Originally it had been painted. Through the heavy rusting you could see traces of dark blue. In the bottom left-hand corner could be read, 16oz. and I thought this might be a tobacco tin, the kind used by pipe smokers.

'Let's see what's inside,' said Matty. 'Come on, Graham, open it!'

We moved our seats to the middle of the cellar, underneath the light bulb, and I handed the box to Matty.

'Go on,' I said. 'This is your discovery, you open it.'

The metal was flaky with decay, but after a few seconds, she inched back the lid and we both saw what looked like a wad of yellow greasy paper.

I was all set to be disappointed; prepared to accept that the contents had been damaged, but Matty delicately touched the old surface and, balancing the box on her knees, gently brought out a package that I now know had been hidden eight decades before.

We were both silent, in that strange light, in that cold place, as she carefully pulled back the paper, and revealed a small book, a pocket watch, a discoloured cigarette case, three coins.

'These were put here by Paul Whitaker,' she said. 'I think he was kept a prisoner – he put his best things in this box. For someone to find.'

The cigarette case was densely worked with curls and curves and in an oval on the front, the letters 'PEW' were joined together.

'Well, there's his initials Matty,' and I pointed to the patterning.

She was busy looking through the pages of the small book.

It was a pocket-sized version of *The Pilgrim's Progress* by John Bunyan, and you could see from the wear that it had been carefully read. Inside the front cover and facing the title page, a J B Roberts, vicar, had written:

To Paul Whitaker for Perseverance, Punctuality
and Attendance at Craybourne Elementary School
July 1912

The watch seemed to be made from steel because the metal back plate was rusted and stained. You could make out the serial number, 30350W, and the government arrow that made it Crown property. The winder no longer turned, and the time was forever fixed at eleven minutes after five.

Matty was quite interested in the coins – two farthings

and an old penny – and I explained the pre-decimal system as well as I was able.

After that, we sat close together on our wooden perches, and I read from the old book the long journey of Christian in his wilderness. Trying to put out of my mind the question as to why anyone might need to hide such a strange assortment in the first place.

It was quite dark outside when we heard the sound of a car approaching, and then the sweep of headlights and the crunch of tyres moving over gravel.

'There aren't any lights on,' I heard Mum say. 'I'm worried Brian.'

Their footsteps came closer. And then Dad spoke.

'There's a light in the cellar. Look!'

We were both at the window, staring up through the grille. I saw Dad's face looking down and shouted out; 'We're down here. We're OK. We're locked in!'

We were released twenty seconds later. It was just after half past five and we'd been down there over three hours.

'Someone came into the house. They locked us in the cellar,' said Matty. 'We were very frightened,' and for a moment, reliving the experience, I thought that she might start crying.

'What happened Graham?' asked Dad, looking anxious.

And I explained.

'Well, we spent a while watching TV and then Matty said she'd like to take a look in the cellar. I didn't see a problem with that so we went down. I was looking for the light switch because I didn't take a torch with me, when Matty heard someone moving about in the house.'

'They were in the kitchen,' she said. 'We heard their feet on the floor. They came towards the cellar. I thought they were going to come down the steps. I thought they were going to get us—' and she started to cry. The huge relief that the ordeal had ended, that we were safe and that life could continue on its course, was overwhelming. And I have to confess I too felt the first surges of emotion since we'd been locked in.

Dad looked around the kitchen, went through into the laundry and checked the back door. Turned the handle; went and looked at the side window.

'Well, there's no sign of a break-in. I'll just call the police – might as well get them on the scene.'

When he'd gone, Mum asked, 'How long was this person in the house? Do you know where they went? Did you get any idea who they might be?'

'We never saw the person. I think there was only one. They were here for about twenty minutes. They spent the time in the study. We heard the computer being used – you know, the sound of the monitor being switched on and the chair being sat on.'

'But we found an old box, Mummy – in the cellar', said Matty, 'and it had coins and a book and other things.'

But Mum seemed distracted by what I'd told her and

when she repeated the information to Dad he went straight back into the study to check for signs of theft.

Police Sergeant Masters was on the scene half an hour later.

He was a tall man with silver hair and bushy eyebrows. He sat at the kitchen table with a mug of tea and listened while I explained what had happened, making notes and occasionally asking questions. When I'd finished, he summarised my version of events.

And then, turning to Mum and Dad, said; 'Well, Mr and Mrs Hayton, to put it mildly, we haven't got a lot to go on. You've got someone who lets themselves into the house, locks the children in the cellar, spends twenty minutes or so in the study, probably using the computer, and then leaves the building.

'No one saw them arrive or depart. The door at the rear of the house is secure and all of the windows are locked. There is no sign of a break-in and you say nothing has been taken. Even if we were to lay our hands on the person who did this thing they could simply turn round and say, 'What crime?'

'Is there anything on the computer that might attract a villain into the house – you know, I don't want to pry, but is there something that someone might wish to steal from you or at least look at?'

'Well, no,' said Dad, straight-faced. 'There's nothing on the hard disk to tempt anyone and the floppies are locked away in the office at work.'

'There are no files or folders or bits of paper, or anything like that lying around?'

'No. I've got to be careful because of the work I do. The office is clean.'

'Well, if anything does occur to you, here's my card and number, give me a call.'

And with that, he placed a broad elastic band round his notebook, drained the last dregs of tea from his mug, and disappeared into the night.

Twenty-two

On frosty Sundays, you can hear the church bells from Brenton Underwood quite clearly. They start up at about 10.30 and persist until 11.00. I sometimes notice their cascades of sound whilst lying on my back, reconciled to the thought of no further sleep.

I mention this because I've recently been asked: 'Where did you put the experience of Paul Whitaker?'

That means, I think, how did I cope with the idea of living in a haunted house, without having religion to fall back on?

We weren't Christians or Buddhists or Muslims or anything, so the matter of the after-life never really came up. Matty still had faith in Father Christmas, but that's different I suppose. And for that matter, where did Matty *put* the experience?

Sometimes she was made very unhappy: I think more because of the sadness of the young man who spoke to her. And I sometimes got the feeling that she just regarded him as another part of her hugely inventive imagination, and that she and I were in some way involved in an elaborate game.

Up until the moment I spoke to Violet Thompson, I tried not to allow the idea of the dead speaking to the living intrude too much into my life. I kind of tricked myself that there were rational explanations for everything and that the only person who had regular contact with Paul Whitaker was a five-year-old.

My conversation with Violet Thompson took a hammer to that view.

Anyway, two restless nights after the cellar experience – and this would be 8th December – I found myself back at school going through the door of room 37 in search of Pyatt.

He was sorting out videos when I arrived, looking for 'something suitable to entertain Year 8'; but at long last, and before sunset, he sat behind his desk, pushed his lunch-box away and said: 'Tell me where we are.'

And then, after the summary, he scratched his ear as if unsure that he'd heard correctly, and came back with: 'And what conclusion do you come to?', his fingers lightly touching the rusted box I'd brought from home.

'I was hoping you might tell me, Mr Pyatt,' I said.

I think that at that moment I wanted someone else to take some responsibility; to make ordinary sense out of extraordinary experience.

He opened the lid and placed the book, cigarette box, watch and coins on the table. And then: 'It would seem, Graham, that if a soldier called Paul Whitaker was staying at Sentinel House in the first war he was either a member of the military police – a redcap – or—'

'He had been arrested?'

'Exactly. And' – pointing to the stuff on his table – 'if it was the latter, if he was some kind of prisoner there, why would he bury his personal possessions in the house? What are we looking at that was so important to him?'

At that point he picked up Bunyan's book and carefully flicked through the pages.

'Mmm, various bits underlined and a couple of marginal comments, but hardly the clue we're looking for. Obviously a Christian, but you'd hardly get locked up for that, unless . . . What I was thinking, and this may be a bit of a long shot, Graham: was Paul Whitaker someone who went through a great change in his way of thinking? Like he found belief – and in some way this got him into trouble? Like – maybe – the work he was being forced to do was suddenly against his principles? Something he couldn't cope with?'

He held the book by its covers and gently pushed them back to expose the gap between the pages and the spine.

'Ah!' he said. 'What have we here?' and he reached into his desk drawer, rummaged for a moment and then produced a pair of tweezers – the kind Mum used to pluck her eyebrows.

He held the book open, horizontally, and slowly extracted a length of paper.

'I think *this* is why he hid the box. This is the great secret that needed to be kept from prying eyes.'

There was a single sheet, unlined and roughly torn along one side. It was covered in closely written pencil script.

Mr Pyatt smoothed it out gently across his desk, and turning to me, said: 'Shall I read it out Graham?'

I nodded and after adjusting his glasses, he began:

11th February 1918

I do not know at which time or place my life shall end, but I know that as God is my guide I have done my duty to my conscience and I dedicate this testament to brothers unknown.

I pledge that everything revealed in these lines was witnessed by myself, Paul Edward Whitaker, Private, Wiltshire Regiment, and that in consequence of my indiscretion it is like that I shall receive stern punishment.

I was placed under close arrest by comrades of the Provost Marshal's office on the 8th January 1918 and charged with treason.

On the 21st I was defendant in a court martial at Sentinel House, New Barton. It was said that I did write a letter to **The Times** *newspaper in London, saying that the work being carried out at New Barton camp was concerned with the making of poisonous gas, and that prisoners in the custody of the Provost Marshal's office were used in experiments to test the results of the substances being manufactured.*

On the advice of Captain King, I admitted the charge as stated in the indictment, but that I pleaded for my good conduct and service record to be taken into account when sentence was being considered.

I own that I have no great hopes for mercy and Captain King advised that I should make my peace with God in the expectation of an absolute sanction.

During front line duty near Arras, I saw how my comrades, their eyes and lips blistered and red, twisted in pain on the dirty ground. How, in the great clouds of poison gas, they spewed blood and choked to their deaths.

My work as clerk at New Barton did not concern me in the making of any ordnance or arranging its use, but to be aware of the suffering of fellow creatures, to be a helpmate in the cause of death, is an abomination I could endure no longer and I gave witness to what I knew.

That my endeavour was fruitless, I can now acknowledge. But if I am to receive a capital sentence, I here entrust these words to the safety of the good earth, and hope that in future, peaceful times, a reader might find lack of regard for narrow patriotism a virtue rather than a treasonous vice.

Paul Whitaker, Private.

Mr Pyatt read the words slowly, sometimes halting when a crease in the paper or the faded hand made understanding difficult. When he had finished, we sat in silence.

I looked across the room and out over the playing field to the houses on the estate. There was a blackheaded gull on sentry duty on top of one of the rugby posts and below, speckling the green, half a dozen others mingled with a flock of starlings.

I thought back to the morning when we had crawled

through the wire and wandered across the rain-swept desolation of the old camp by Wilson's Wood. The very place where gas experiments had been carried out on British prisoners. And where one young man broke ranks and took their part.

I thought too of the letters written in the condensation of my window, the word 'Gas' bleeding away on the glass.

'An extraordinary story,' said Mr Pyatt eventually. 'I don't suppose Miss Thompson got any of that from the Ministry of Defence.'

'What do you think happened to him?' I said.

My Pyatt paused, touching the paper lightly with his forefinger. 'I don't know Graham. He was put on trial for his life and he confessed to a very serious offence. He would have been a lucky man to have survived. I think you'll have to wait until you see Miss Thompson on Friday. I have a hunch that she might hold a vital piece of the puzzle.'

Twenty-three

It's still difficult to get the twenty-four hours surrounding that next Thursday straight.

When I go through the sequence I can remember that 10th December was overcast and grey from start to finish. That we had a cross-country run in the afternoon and that I discovered an uneaten cheese sandwich in my bag on the way home.

I can remember eating it whilst watching the rain, like beads of sweat, stream against the passing windows of the bus.

Of course it was the day of the American visitors and the eve of Dad's great sales convention. Dad had been gone an hour by the time I had sat down to breakfast that morning and Matty had spent the meal stirring great puddles of syrup into her porridge before deciding she didn't want it after all.

The Americans were due at 8.30, and although the original idea was that I would take part in the meal, Dad thought it would be easier on my social skills, and give the occasion greater focus, if I ate at the conventional hour of

5.30, got introduced to the 'dudes from across the pond' and then spent some time in my room. Like the rest of the evening.

I wasn't devastated by the change of plans, although it did seem crazy to have to get dressed in my new jacket and airstream trousers just for a few moments of touching base.

Mum wasn't particularly bothered by the prospect of VIPs. Once she'd worked out that the evening might have an Italian flavour, she got set on working through pasta recipes in her various cook books. During that week, the break-in forgotten, she'd suddenly interrupt stuff we were doing – homework or computer programming; watching TV or eating supper – and say, 'What do you think of this? Do you think it might be a bit too much as a starter?'

And she'd explain what the dish involved and how it contrasted to the projected main course, and so-on and so forth.

My suggestion: 'Mum, why don't you do a couple of pizzas and some salad with that purply coloured lettuce? Everyone likes pizza. Have a few bottles of wine to warm the conversation. That'll be great.'

All this met with five seconds of silenzio. And then the big freeze-out: 'No, no, Graham. You simply don't understand. This is an important occasion for your father – well, for all of us, and we want it to be great success.'

So maybe my earlier observation about Mum being unconcerned was three streets wide of the mark. Looking back over it now, I guess that whole week was filled with tension. What with the Americans arriving and the sales convention. The fact that the locks on the doors front and back were being replaced and a security light installed in the garden. And the fact that I woke two nights in a row, convinced there was something wrong in the house.

Yet, on that Thursday, and for the last time, I sat in Dad's bathroom and chatted to him whilst he got shaved: I listened to the sound of the blade scraping over his chin and the occasional splash of water, trying to find a way to open a conversation.

'Odd, really, that someone who works in high tech should use old technology to shave with.'

He looked down at me for a second, perhaps wondering whether I was going to ask him for a loan. Neither of us sensing that this was the beginning of the end.

'Well, you can't beat it, can you?' he said, and then resumed scraping. 'Learnt this at my father's knee. Something comforting about it.' He splashed the razor into the water. 'Quality thinking time this, you know!'

'I know that the sales thing you're involved in is important for the company and everything, but doesn't it bother you that you might be sort of – well – helping in some war effort that might lead—'

'– to innocent lives being lost? Arms sales overseas? That kind of thing? Excuse me one second,' and he bent over the sink to splash water over his cheeks.

'Sure I do. Yes!' He reached down and picked up a towel. 'But that kind of thinking goes nowhere. If it wasn't me, it would be someone else, but more to the point, the selling of arms is quite well controlled nowadays, you know. Don't worry about it!'

He rinsed his hands under the tap, ruffled my hair and pushed past me into another future.

The Americans rolled up at twenty to nine in one of those large cross-country-style vehicles, you know, high axle and large treads.

They were called Jeff and Tom. Jeff was shiny bald with large, light-reflecting teeth and Tom was tall and thin, with a straggly moustache and said 'Howdy' as if he'd walked in off the streets of Abilene.

Although I never got the chance to check back with Mum – because everything kind of fell apart after that – I remember feeling how big and confident and well, sort of exotic they were. Like they'd stepped out of the frame of some TV programme. And I suppose that's because most people's experience of Americans is through films and news bulletins. They were like huge tropical butterflies that had just flopped in from the coast.

I did my best to remain inconspicuous so that I could hang around and gawp, but come ten past nine Mum said that the meal was only five minutes away from blast-off, so I said goodnight and shuffled off to flick through a book on UFOs.

From my perspective, that part of the evening went well. Dad was enthusing about some software he'd just encountered; the Americans, particularly Tom, were fascinated by British place-names.

'And how do you pronounce Sal-is-bury?'

And Mum was busy with the cannelloni in the kitchen.

Later Dad gave the visitors a preview of the video on the StarRaider and I was surprised that Matty didn't stir and start creating. The twin engines boomed and roared up the stairs, gunned and twisted in a tight turn past the bookshelf before screaming out low over the carpet.

After the air display, I discarded the text on aliens and, as I recall, crashed into sleep listening to an old Frank Zappa soundtrack, filched from the music room at school. I woke up to something entirely different.

To begin with I had that moment of dislocation you get when you stay in someone else's place and you open your eyes and wonder where you are. It was quite dark in the room – the low cloud-base totally cut off any lurking rays from the moon – and the house seemed quiet.

But something wasn't right – as if the bed was at the wrong angle or a door was banging. I felt cold and the air was thick with expectation. And then, in the distance, but coming closer, the tramp tramp of marching feet. Hundreds of men pounding the ground.

I had in mind Dad's earlier observation about an aural mirage – sound waves carried over great distances on clear nights. But this wasn't like that. The noise got closer, seemed to hang in the air and fade momentarily, and then would rush on again. Coming towards us like the incoming tide pushing up a beach.

Closer and closer.

Looking back it was hypnotic in a way: like listening to a steam engine heading in from a great distance. The dense weight of hundreds of boots crashing in unison; the pounding pistons of some great machine.

But soon, noise filled the room, filled the house. And everything seemed to be shaking. I could hear stuff on my shelves – a model of the *QE II*, a scattering of fossils from a field trip – start to vibrate, like the ground beneath us was beginning to shift and turn.

There was a cry from along the corridor. There was a crash from downstairs and then the whole parade was on us, hammering through the house; bursting through the walls and doors like the rush of the sea smashing sand defences built by a child.

There were lights on in the corridor and a cascade of noise below – breaking wood and wrenching metal. A great screaming wash of sound.

And then, as I heard footsteps on the stairs, there was silence. Like one second there's a force nine gale breaking up the sea and the next the water is as still as a millpond. Like the spasm of grief you get from children followed by the abrupt quiet once a source of comfort has been found.

Matty was crying; and Dad's voice came from somewhere down below: 'This is unbelievable. Kate, you'd better come and have a look.'

Clear through the house, through the study, through the lounge, a path had been driven. The computer table was in two pieces, upended like a torpedoed ship, and the monitor was on its side, a massive crack splintering the glass.

Books and files littered the floor and a pool of black ink glistened on the carpet.

The smash-up in the lounge – the coffee table thrown against one of the walls, both armchairs upended, yesterday's vase of flowers shattered across the hearth, a jagged line cracking the paper on the far wall – mirrored the wreckage in the study.

In both rooms, the pattern was clear: everything had been driven to one side. The walls were intact, but a path had broken through the house as clearly as a troop of soldiers blazing a trail in the Burmese jungle.

Dad lifted the phone in the hall, had just got to the second 9 in the sequence when the sound of an approaching car made him pause. We saw the headlights of a vehicle entering our drive and then the front door bell started to ring.

It was the police.

'Mr Hayton?' asked the first officer, and I noticed a second car waiting in the road outside.

'Yes,' said Dad, obviously bemused.

'We'd like you to get dressed and accompany us to Craybourne police station. I'm arresting you for disclosing information classified under Section 2 of the 1989 Official Secrets Act.'

Twenty-four

Friday started clear and cold and stayed that way.

My hands felt the chill as I pedalled down the road into New Barton, towards Underwood Lane.

It was gone eleven but no one was about and only the smoke from one of the alms houses gave the impression of life. Everything else was listless and still.

The police had arrived at just gone 2.30. The officers glanced at the wreckage on the ground floor and then passed an instruction to a colleague back at Craybourne.

But the second group didn't appear until four and after inspecting the outside of the house and asking obvious questions went away as puzzled as the rest of us. A fingerprint check was to be made during normal working hours.

I stopped the bike by the stream and watched the water slip past a piece of rotting chestnut. It had been there since October, since some kids had pelted the tree to give up its clutch of conkers. The leaves on the branch were long gone and as the water flowed past so the wood moved gently in the current.

We weren't able to sort out the confusion in the lounge and study. The police were very clear that both areas were to be subject to further investigation by the Special Branch. Each door was locked and sealed, a procedure that added a further layer of nightmare, as if we were being gradually evicted from our own home.

At half past nine, Mum called Craybourne station. There was a long delay whilst she was transferred from section to section, before: 'I see. And we can't come over and visit him?'

'He's being held for questioning,' she said when she replaced the receiver. There were dark smudges beneath her eyes; a strand of hair had come adrift and hung across her face.

'They won't let me visit him. Arthur Bellamy, our solicitor, has been to find out what's going on.'

We sat in the kitchen and drank coffee. I think we were both hoping that the front door would suddenly open, Dad would walk in and everything would carry on as before. Dad would say something like: 'Incredible mistake. Thought I was someone else. Now, is that coffee I smell?'

But of course, it wasn't like that. When Bellamy phoned it was to relay the coarse facts of the case. I sat at the top of the stairs with Matty, trying to make sense of the conversation:

'But that's plainly ridiculous. Have they considered his record with Spere?'

'I know Mr Bellamy—'

'Yes, but why would he want to do that? Even I can see—'

'So we'll be able to visit him this afternoon? This evening? For heaven's sake! This *is* ridiculous!'

She was standing in the kitchen looking out over the garden when we went down. Her voice was tired and flat. 'Mr Bellamy says that the operating details of the StarRaider aircraft – the software Dad was working on for Spere – have been published on the internet. The American company that wanted the technology has discovered this and has broken off negotiations.'

She paused, as if trying to comprehend what she'd just said.

'Because of the nature of the work Dad was engaged on, any publication of this information is strictly against the Official Secrets Act. Dad signed the act when he went to work for Spere, so he was aware of his obligations—'

'But Dad wouldn't have—' I began.

'No. He's denied all knowledge of what has happened, but the police say that they have traced back from the website and all paths lead to this door. They say there's absolutely no doubt that the source of the information – how it got on to the internet – was from our number.'

The white Ford was parked outside John's house, and I dutifully propped my bike against the fence.

Looking back from this distance, I think I acted in that way because I simply couldn't stand hanging around the house waiting for nothing to happen. There was no point in going to school and after a while there are few variations of 'It'll be all right' before you feel that the script has simply run out.

There was no sound from Mr Thomas's workshop. But the padlock hung loose from the hasp, so I gave the door a more confident rap than I felt.

There were a couple of seconds' silence and then the door pushed open and he stood looking down at me, as if annoyed at being interrupted. There was a paintbrush in his right hand and the smell of varnish hung in the air.

'Ah, Graham, isn't it?' he said. 'Well, come in. What can I do for you?'

'That's difficult, Mr Thomas. It's a complicated story—'

'Well, take a seat – there, grab that stool. Yes that's it. You don't mind if I carry on with this do you? Don't want to leave a tide mark by stopping and starting.'

He went back to painting the body of the horse, stroking the wet varnish into the wood.

'Mr Thomas,' I said, conscious that within minutes he'd be turfing me out of his shed with a curse.

'Mr Thomas, my father was arrested during the night.'

He carried on with his work, dipping the brush into the tin and carefully following the grain.

'The police say that he released secret information about the StarRaider project on to the internet and that he's being charged under the Official Secrets Act.'

He refreshed his brush, listening. I looked around the

workshop, noticing for the first time the several carved heads that hung on the walls at the back, waiting to be attached to bodies.

Silence filled the air like dust.

He said, turning round, 'I'm sorry to hear about your dad – ah, Graham – but what has this got to do with me?'

'Mr Thomas,' I started again. 'You've visited our house and you know the kind of people we are. Do you think it likely that my dad would have done such a thing?'

He finished the right hind leg, wiped the varnish from the brush, and then placed it in a jar of water. He took a cloth, poured some turps onto it and rubbed his hands.

'Do you think I had something to do with this, ah, criminal act?'

'I don't know Mr Thomas. I–I think you might know more than you're saying to me.'

I thought at that moment he was going to lose his temper, that he would start shouting and that I'd have simply wasted my time and caused more trouble. And that the police would be wanting to know why I'd interfered with the investigation.

'Let me see,' he said, leaning against the doorpost. 'You'll have noticed, I expect, the special way I have of smiling?' He pointed to the curious, lopsided twist to his face.

'I wasn't born like that, Graham. It wasn't some kind of genetic inheritance from my mam or dad. But I was lucky. I was caught by a high-velocity round from a rifle. The bullet clipped a muscle as it passed by at twenty-two hundred feet a second. My pal, standing next to me, wasn't so fortunate. The metal that caught him took away a vertebrae at the base of his spine. Took him to the ground quicker than an axed tree.

'And the pathetic thing was, as he lay in the mud, he tried to get up. The top half of his body straining to make his legs work. But of course they didn't because communications traffic from base HQ had been severed.

'He got a good pension and waltzes around in a super-dooper wheelchair and everything, but you see it's not the same. Not with his being a keen rugby player and athlete. Kind of spoiled that.

'That was all years ago, in the Falklands – during the war between Britain and Argentina in the eighties. The crazy thing about it was that my pal was hit with a bullet manufactured in London, and I expect that I was grazed by metal machined in the same place.'

'But—' I began.

'I mean years ago the people who made the swords and the bows and the arrows, they were probably familiar with the effects of their craft. They knew that if you hit someone hard enough with a sword, you'll take an arm clean away, chop a great wedge out of a body, but if you're in front of a monitor all day – well, you might as well be putting together the code for a games machine.'

'Mr Thomas,' I said again. 'I understand all this. He was working on software for a European defence aircraft. It wasn't designed for export as far as I know. Simply to protect Britain against invaders.'

He looked at me sharply, and then pulled a handkerchief from his pocket and blew his nose.

'You don't believe that, do you?'

He spoke softly and at that moment I felt a great surge of emotion, like a rising tide that had been held back.

'No,' I said quietly.

'Things are difficult for all of us, Graham,' he said eventually. 'But when you see great wrongs being done and stand aside, surely you're as guilty as the person committing that offence?'

He paused and rubbed his eyes as if trying to get something straight.

'Look, you're a young man and I know that you're acting as the local attorney on behalf of your father. I know that he's a clever man and that he was hired by the company to provide the brains for this wonderful aeroplane.

'But I haven't much to say that will be of comfort to you Graham. Your dad sold his skills on the market. The technology he was working on will be used to kill people in the Third World – mums and dads, aunties and uncles, babies and children – thousands of miles from comfy New Barton.'

And at that moment, as we talked in the cold of his workshop, I got the feeling that Mr Thomas had been through all these arguments before. The bullet that had caught his face in the Falklands War, the round fired by the

Argentine soldier, had been made in Britain, and was still hurtling through the air. Last night it had struck Dad.

'Some version of that aeroplane will be exported to a dictatorship abroad who will use it to slaughter whoever happens to be the particular enemy at the time. Who can say that it's wrong to try and stop that?'

He picked up the tin of varnish and carefully replaced the lid.

'There's nothing I can do for you Graham,' he said.

Twenty-five

Violet Thompson was short and heavily stooped and she took an age getting to the front door of her house. You could hear the slow shuffle and pause as she came down the corridor.

Her hair was thin and pure white and her eyes blue and direct.

'Yes, what is it?' she asked, looking up at me.

'Miss Thompson, my name's Graham Hayton.'

'Ah, the boy who's doing the research? You'd better come in.'

I hadn't planned to stop. But because everything was turned around at home I didn't think afternoon tea was going to be a strong possibility. Yet if she'd been busy making seed cake then the least I could do was to call in and explain something of the situation.

The house – in the middle of the terrace – was a small two-bedroomed affair. Red brick mixed with flint as was the local custom.

I followed her instruction and placed my jacket on a hook in the hall and then went into the lounge – a tiny area filled with books and framed watercolours. There was a brisk fire burning and just room for a couple of armchairs and a coffee table.

'I'm not expecting you at this time am I?' she asked anxiously, as if concerned that the cold fingers of dementia had touched her world.

'No, no. I'm due at half past four Miss Thompson but there's been a – well – a disaster at home and – well – I have to be on hand to help out should the need arise.'

'But you'll take a cup of tea?'

'Yes. Thanks.'

On any other day I'd have been less abrupt, less withdrawn. I found the effort of making conversation as hard as running any cross-country against the clock. All the time I was in that small house – which smelled of old flowers and furniture polish – I was also wondering what was going on at home.

I followed her into the kitchen and for several minutes, as we waited for the kettle to sort itself out, listened to her talk about her house and the village and the research she had once completed. She used to teach in the old school and the pamphlet on New Barton was the first project of her retirement.

'You see, there weren't any leisure centres or aerobics classes in those days, fortunately, so I was quite happy to check parish records and interview people through newspaper advertisements. I know that it's not very substantial but it took me the best part of two years to put together.

‘I had a couple of hundred copies printed and sold about half that number through the bookshop in Craybourne. If I’d had more money I’d have included some photographs of the people I met and the buildings I described.’

She paused and sipped from her cup.

‘And you’re living in Sentinel House you say?’

‘Yes. We moved in last October.’

‘You said there’d been some disaster at home. Not tragic, I hope?’

‘No. Not tragic. But, well – it’s difficult to explain Miss Thompson.’

‘That’s all right dear. It’s none of my business. But perhaps I can help you with your interest in Sentinel House,’ and she reached under the coffee table and pulled out a faded blue folder.

‘After I published my pamphlet on the village, several people wrote, saying how much they’d enjoyed the work. Sometimes they corrected mistakes I’d made and sometimes they provided additional bits of information – just in case I might consider bringing out another edition.

‘Well, although I did think about putting together a revised version of the history, I never got round to it. The original impulse seemed to have died, and it was never done. But – and more to the point of your visit – about a year after the pamphlet had been in circulation, I received a letter from an Elizabeth Holroyd in Beauminster. She’d been sent the pamphlet by her daughter who lived in our part of the world.

'Elizabeth was well into her eighties at that time but she had once worked as a serving maid in the kitchen at Sentinel House when it was the Provost Marshal's headquarters, and furthermore, she was courting a sergeant who worked up the hill at the old camp.'

At this point she opened the file and turned over several sheets of lined paper until she came to an envelope.

'This is what I think you might find of interest in your research,' and she passed the envelope over, commenting, 'It was a sad business.'

The writer had used a biro and had been taught in the copperplate manner – all loops and curves. But over the years, the style had deteriorated and become ragged, like an old hedge that had been neglected and allowed to develop its own outgrowths and wild shape. Consequently it was sometimes difficult to get the meaning of a passage and I found myself reading whole pages over again in order to pick up the narrative.

This extract commences halfway down the third page:

I was appointed kitchen maid in the Provost Marshal's office at Sentinel House in the autumn of 1917.

The soldiers were known as red caps on account of the distinctive band they wore on their uniform hats. They served as the army's police force.

In the early part of 1918 a soldier was brought into Sentinel House and imprisoned in one of the basement cells. I can remember this quite clearly because he was the subject of a lot of talk by the officers in the place, and we gathered that he'd committed a serious offence and that he was to be put on trial for it – a court martial in fact.

He was served meals like everyone else, the food being taken down to him by the duty guard. Then one day, sometime in February I would have thought, I was asked to make a seed cake for the prisoner. The cook was ill at the time and I remember most particular that the cake had to be ready by teatime on a Wednesday.

Well, that wasn't a great hardship, although I thought it odd that a fellow who had been locked away for the past month and given a mighty plain diet might now be indulged with a most particular confection.

To get to the point, the cake was made and he was given a slice on the Wednesday, as per instruction and then blow me, he vanishes from the place.

'What is the prisoner having for lunch?' I asked the next day and I was told that he'd left.

Well, in time of war, you got used to odd things happening. Your job was to carry out orders and do your duty.

Shortly after this, that Easter, I started courting with a sergeant from the camp, Frank Holroyd. He never liked to talk about his work, but years after when we'd been married and had two babies with a third on the way, Frank told me about an incident that had taken place during the war.

He felt bad about what had happened and as he told the story he had difficulty in containing his emotion.

All the soldiers were roused at seven one morning and

made to stand around three-quarters of the parade ground. A further platoon of nine stood within the square, with their rifles in the shoulder arms position.

Presently a lorry drew up, some men jumped down from the back and dragged a third onto the ground. Frank said that they were none too gentle with this creature, but treated him as if he were a particularly troublesome bag of spuds.

This third soldier had his hands tied behind him and he was led, head down, onto the parade ground, so that all the assembled could see his plight.

Frank said that everyone was filled with foreboding at this, because they recognised that the prisoner was Private Whitaker, who had until recently been one of their number and was friendly with several.

When young Whitaker was situated at the open end of the square, next to a wooden chair placed for the purpose, the Sergeant Major brought the company to attention and one of the officers addressed the parade.

He told them that it was his duty to communicate the sentence of the recent court martial held on Private Whitaker and to ensure that it was carried out to the satisfaction of the law and in favour of military discipline.

Well, the upshot was that Whitaker had been sentenced to death by firing squad for betraying his country and that this sentence had been confirmed by various generals and big wigs in the army. There was no court of appeal or anything like that.

They dragged Whitaker to the chair and quickly bound

him hand and foot, dropped a black bag over his head and pinned a piece of white cloth to his chest.

The nine soldiers who had come equipped with rifles took their aim and at the signal of the officer – he brought down his swagger stick – fired a volley into the heart of the young man.

Frank said that the force of the bullets, ripping into his body, knocked him sideways, and that he continued to jerk and move for some minutes after the spirit had passed from him.

And as he lay there, covered in blood, so the Colonel told the men that justice had been done and that this was to be seen as a warning to anyone else who had treasonous thoughts on their mind.

By comparing times and dates it was obvious that the young man who had been imprisoned at Sentinel House was the same Paul Whitaker who had been so brutally killed up on the hill.

I believe that his grave can be found in the churchyard at Tydeworth camp.

Frank told me that it was the most disgraceful act he witnessed during his three years in the army and that it made him ashamed to wear the King's uniform.

As I sat there, with the letter in my hand, before Miss Thompson and that roaring fire, I thought back over the various moments during those few weeks that winter; thought back over the events that had taken place eighty years before, and wondered yet again how far the past had stretched out a hand to touch the present. I thought too of those words we'd uncovered in the cellar:

'To be aware of the suffering of fellow creatures, to be a helpmate in the cause of death, is an abomination I could endure no longer and I gave witness to what I knew.'

Twenty-six

'Mr Hayton, I wonder if you might glance over this document. Now could you explain to the court what we are looking at?'

'It's a copy of the Official Secrets Act.'

'Ah. And what is that?'

'It's a law designed to safeguard the security of the country.'

' "To safeguard the security of the country!" Exactly so, Mr Hayton. The Official Secrets Act is signed by people who work in secret areas. By signing it they promise not to reveal those secrets to anyone else. Isn't that so, Mr Hayton?'

'Yes.'

'And were the severe penalties for breaking the Act explained to you?'

'Yes.'

'Yes. So why did you have to sign the document when you took your job at Spere Electronics?'

'Because I was involved in designing computer software that was being developed for use in an advanced fighter aircraft.'

'And the British government – and other European

governments for that matter – wouldn't want information about this aircraft – technical information about how it flies – to be widely known?'

'No.'

'So would you like to tell the court how such technical information was made available on the internet? How it could be accessed by *anyone* plugging into a website called – ah – Lamplight? And how your own email address was given as the contact for further enquiries?'

'I don't know. I never passed on any information over the internet. Or made copies of classified inform—'

'But you have already pleaded guilty to breaking one section of the Official Secrets Act: you've already told this court that you were in the habit of taking computer disks home.'

'Yes, but—'

'And the email address publicised on the internet is yours?'

'Yes.'

'What I wonder, Mr Hayton, is how you can still maintain your innocence?'

We had to wait five months for the trial at Craybourne Crown Court. Five months before the press recorded the way Roger Carlyle QC tore gaping wounds in Dad's defence. I was a mere fifty metres from him, whilst all this was going on. It might have been 2,000 kilometres. I sat on a bench outside Court Number 2 watching the black movement of clerks and lawyers.

'It's because you're a defence witness, young man,' said Mr Bellamy, puffing on his cigar. 'Got to wait your turn.'

The press had arrived immediately news broke about Dad's arrest.

I'd just got to the bend on Potters Road, before our house, when I saw the parked cars and groups of people in front of the fence. A film crew was unloading from the side of a van and a blonde-haired woman came out of the gate. Even from a distance you could hear their chat and laughter. Several were drinking from the lids of vacuum flasks and a man in a leather jacket was eating a sandwich as he talked to his friend.

They stopped what they were doing as I pedalled up the road. Then there was the lightning of flash bulbs and someone pushed a microphone into my face.

'It's Graham, isn't it?' said this man with a short beard and thin face, and someone grabbed my arm and a third called out: 'What do you know about your Dad, Graham?' and 'Do you think he's a spy?'

And then I broke free and ran the bike down the side of the house, shaking off further shouts like a cloud of summer flies.

'They've been here for the last hour,' said Mum. 'I've had to switch on the answerphone because of the number of calls we were getting. We've been offered thousands of pounds by the newspapers to tell our story.'

Matty was at the kitchen table, listening. She had a book open and was messily colouring a picture of a farmyard.

'Is there any—'

'News?' Mum interrupted, moving to the sink to fill the kettle. 'Yes. Plenty. It's the main item on TV and radio. There's even been a statement from the American government saying that they have every confidence that Britain will deal with this serious breach of security.'

'Daddy didn't do anything wrong,' said Matty, her tongue lolling out in concentration. 'He's a–a good man.'

'No, I didn't—'

'I know – forgive me,' Mum said, coming across the kitchen and touching my arm. 'You wondered if we'd heard from the police not whether we're on *Panorama*.'

She leaned against the chest unit by the cooker.

'You know, Graham, I haven't had a cigarette in sixteen years, and yet if one of those goons' – and she gestured towards the front of the house – 'came in and offered me one I think I'd smoke the whole packet.'

I let the silence gather so that all we could hear was the steady scrape of Matty's felts. I never really thought about it then, but on reflection I suppose she was comforting herself, working on an activity that would keep demons away.

'We can see Dad at six o'clock this evening. Arthur Bellamy says that he's going to appear before a magistrate this afternoon and that the police are likely to oppose bail.'

'Which means—' I began.

Mum shut me up with a look. Although events were

unravelling at frightening speed, she still wanted to protect Matty from the certainty that Dad was going to spend the next few months locked in a cell whilst awaiting trial.

That lunchtime, we sat and stirred tomato soup around our bowls. It was as though all our lives had been suspended: like we'd taken a wrong turning somewhere and had found ourselves facing a brick wall, unable to get back to the main road.

At one stage, Mum leapt up from her seat, dragged the back door open and ran out, shouting to a photographer, 'Get out of our garden. If you trespass again I'll call the police.'

And all the time, Matty sat quietly, nibbling a piece of bread and sipping her soup. She spoke only once, but when Mum came back inside and closed the door, she asked: 'Will Daddy be coming home soon?'

We were at the police station in Craybourne a shade before ten to six. Whilst Mum went down a brightly lit corridor with a police officer, Matty and myself waited in Interview Room 2. It was very cramped and bare: a small table and three chairs; the walls covered in writing. In some bizarre way it reminded me of the hut in the camp at Wilson's Wood. Although there were few drawings on view, the place was stamped with unhappiness and desperation. A place where people tried to lie their way back to freedom.

After about half an hour, and after I'd read a couple of

picture-books, we were led down a corridor and into Room 32. Dad rose as we entered and clutched at Matty who rushed to wrap her arms around him. He looked at me over the top of Matty's head and I could see that he was trying to control his emotions – you know, the ones that are pressing you to cry but you realise you mustn't, so that the effort robs you of speech and leaves you with an ache in your throat.

'Daddy's all right,' said Mum, standing up from her chair next to the table. 'They've been very nice to him and Mr Bellamy has arranged for a special lawyer to come down from London so that Daddy can come home as soon as possible.'

We didn't stay long and not a lot was said. Dad worked hard to ask us questions and made jokes about the journalists and photographers, but you could see that he was exhausted after the sleepless night, the hours of questioning, the shock of the arrest. The fact that his tie had been taken away was a reminder that he was no longer able to do as he wished.

And so the months passed.

Bail was opposed; we were all interviewed by the police, including Matty – and as winter thawed into spring and the days lengthened to summer, Dad was kept in a cell at Borough Bridge Prison.

Sometimes Mum went to see him on her own, sometimes all three of us drove the thirty miles across Hampshire. They were long, miserable months. After the first weeks of press interest and an explosion of fascination at school, a kind of dreary routine took over. Lesson followed lesson and although I would occasionally go and chat to Pyatt, each day school slid further down my list of priorities. I sometimes saw John Franklin, but I had no interest in chewing the fat at break, even less in going round at weekends.

Each Tuesday and Saturday we could see Dad; Thursday night we all went to the supermarket and on Sundays we helped clean the house.

Because Dad's salary had been frozen by Spere (until the result of the trial was known), Mum put her name on the county register of supply teachers. Several days a week she dropped Matty off at a childminder's in the village and then hurtled down the lanes to whichever secondary school had hired her services.

Of all of us, I think Matty took the sudden disappearance of Dad the hardest. She would call out in the night complaining of a stomach ache or would wake up screaming from a nightmare. Often she would go into Mum's room before six, crying that she didn't like Mrs Hilliard, the minder, and that they were nasty to her at school.

I suppose with everything else going on, it was natural that Mum should seek help from our GP, who referred us to Doctor Davies at the family guidance clinic.

That side of it – talking to the psychologist – didn't really bother me at the time: I think Mum and myself were too tuned in to the possibility that not only had Dad been suspended by Spere but that he was facing years in prison.

Twenty-seven

'I am innocent because I *never* transmitted the source codes or anything else relating to the StarRaider on the internet.'

'And yet, according to the witness statement obtained from your managing director, Mr Fletcher, there are aspects of the code that only *you* were working on. Isn't that so?'

'Yes.'

'So, your honour, ladies and gentlemen of the jury, the information that found its way on to the internet could only have been produced by Mr Hayton. No one else had access to the work. And no one else had the same email address.

'No further questions, your honour.'

The trial had started at ten that morning in May. We'd left early because of road works just before the Shaftesbury junction, and arrived with forty minutes to spare.

Mum and myself had few words to say as we followed the stop-go tail lights into Craybourne. There had been a mention of the trial on the nine o'clock news bulletin and I suspect an outline of the case appeared in most of the newspapers, but none of us were interested in what the press had to say. A resentful Matty, clutching her pink rabbit, was dropped off at Mrs Hilliard's.

Mr Bellamy had hired Christopher Dyer QC from London to act as our defence advocate.

'He'll do a thorough job, Mrs Hayton,' Bellamy said the week before the trial. 'It's not as bad as you might think,' and he patted Mum's arm as he showed us to the door.

He'd spent the session explaining the rules that would operate throughout the trial so that we could understand what was going on during the various stages. It was very like a play, with everyone cast into different roles, taking turns to perform in character.

The serious questioning of Dad by the prosecution occurred on the afternoon of the first day. It had followed statements by Dad's boss, Mr Fletcher, and by a Mr Simon Glover who had been introduced to the court as an expert witness for the prosecution. His job was to show the jury how the magic of the internet worked – how you got the genie out of the bottle, so to speak.

I suppose for the audience in that legal theatre it would have been great entertainment – after the prosecution build-up – to actually *see* what the crime looked like on a website halfway round the world, but it wasn't great TV if you knew that Exhibit A had the power to turn the key on your life.

According to Mum, speaking to me over a dinner that

neither of us ate, Glover was a young man in his twenties who wore his hair in a pony-tail.

'It sat on his shoulders,' she said, 'like a dead rat.' He had a thin voice and a cough that broke up his speech.

'He wasn't called straight away,' she said. 'The prosecution wanted a short adjournment. A couple of men came in and put up a screen and pushed in the electronic boxes – you know, PC and projector and so forth.' She looked away, staring out through the kitchen window to the garden wall and the ivy glistening in the pale light.

'The prosecution QC, Mr Carlyle, said that he wanted the jury to see for themselves how the internet worked. How easy it was to send messages to the States.

'Then of course they brought in the weedy Simon Glover who had to be reminded on two occasions to speak up because the court microphone wasn't recording what he was saying.'

Again she stopped and I was conscious of how worn – how frayed – she looked. The fading light didn't help, but her grey eyes shone like broken glass; her lipstick had leached into her skin.

I guess the jury must have been really wired up by the time Mr Carlyle put Glover through his paces. They'd pulled up a search engine as a start – probably TashKent from Mum's description – and then before going any further, Carlyle turned to the jury and said: 'So let us see, ladies and gentlemen of the jury, what the work of a traitor looks like. Indeed, let us see where the top secret information entrusted to the care of Brian Hayton ended up.

'Could you please type in StarRaider?'

I could only imagine the dry-mouthed anticipation that would have met that request, people straining in their seats to get a better look at the screen.

And then of course, three or four seconds later, the handful of options appeared, including:

Development

Government policy

History

and

Operating codes

And then after Carlyle had allowed the tension to stretch a little: 'Operating codes.'

There was complete silence in court during this sequence of events, and nobody spoke when the following text, blue on white, flashed across four thousand miles and hung a guilty sign on the screen in Court Number 2. For the secret that Lamplight gave to the world went like this: 'The following lines contain source code for the StarRaider avionics system. This information has been made available to the public in the interest of world peace. For an update contact: hayton@sentinel.boulder.co.uk.'

There then appeared lines and lines and lines of what might have been hieroglyphics.

The binary black magic.

Twenty-eight

We had to wait until the third day for our interrogation.

It was one of those typically English spring mornings – not clear blue skies, swallows and cowslips, but thick wads of cloud, steady rain and traffic stalled on the dual carriageway. I sat in the back of the car, next to Matty, re-reading Dad's letter. It had been written on Monday night, and when I look at it now I can feel once again the sense of foreboding – that the earnest hope expressed would not be fulfilled. It wasn't a comfort as we crawled into Craybourne: it added to the misery because I guess it emphasised everything that might be thrown away.

Dear Graham

I'm not in a position to talk to you as I would have liked, but I want to apologise for getting you involved in this drama. I'm quite sure that you'll just be asked to talk about the time you and Matty were locked in the cellar – and of course the prosecution will want you to say that I brought the wretched computer disks home on a regular basis. Just tell the truth in your own way and I know the jury will believe in what they hear.

This has been a terrible – frightening – experience for us all, although I'm quite sure that at some stage we'll be able to look back and find some value in it.

During these past few months I've had plenty of time to think about our lives – the good and the not so wonderful. And I suppose that now mine has been put on hold, I can regret lost opportunities.

When I was a child I went with a friend to a nearby level crossing and for whole days during one summer we spent our time collecting the numbers of passing trains. Somewhere in the attic you'll find those notebooks.

I confess that I can still remember the sense of excitement I felt when we heard the whine of the rails before the gate swung across the road. And then the rush of the passing train. At the end of the day there were all those pages filled with neat columns of numbers and a sense of a job well done.

It was like ordering the world into a comfortable, controllable shape.

I've never thought back to that time until today, when Mr Glover called up the website and we could see the lines of computer code that had come from my disks. As I looked at the screen I couldn't help wondering whether I hadn't spent my life waiting for passing trains.

This is a bit deep, but perhaps if I'm given a second chance we might go to Stamford Bridge together and see the greatest team in the world do their stuff.

With love

Your Dad.

As everyone now knows, Matty was interviewed after lunch on Wednesday afternoon. Mr Bellamy and Mr Dyer felt that her testimony about what had happened during our afternoon in the cellar would appeal to the jury. There had never been a dispute about the incident, but Matty's innocence would add credibility to the case: she would speak the truth.

Because of her age it was arranged for her to sit with Mum in a counselling room and be videoed with a colleague of Mr Dyer's. The film of the interview to be transmitted live into the court.

But this was later, after my own ordeal under cross-examination.

Although Mr Bellamy had explained how everything worked in the court days before the trial opened, having to sit in the long corridor that Wednesday morning, watching and not seeing the cars filtering through on to the Shaftesbury road, I think I would have changed places with the greasy youth begging coins in the underpass.

For forty minutes I had to wait, without knowing when the pale door into the large room would swing back, and the summons to take the stand would be made. Having to tell my story according to the ritual of question and answer; aware of Mum in the visitors' area; the cluster of lawyers and clerks; the curious jury opposite; the press behind; the judge Mr Wingate to my left. And to my right, his face stretched and grey, my father.

But then suddenly it was 'Mr Hayton?' and I was in the witness box, and repeating after the clerk the words:'I swear by almighty God that the evidence I shall give shall be the truth, the whole truth, and nothing but the truth.'

And later still, once I had explained to Mr Dyer what had taken place in the cellar, I stood looking at the face of the prosecuting counsel, Mr Roger Carlyle, who rose thoughtfully from his chair and approached with a frown creasing his forehead.

'Mr Hayton,' he began. 'You have told the jury that on the afternoon of 6th December last year you went down into the cellar of your house. Is that correct?'

'Yes.'

'How long were you in the cellar, with your sister, Mathilda, before you heard the sound of someone walking through your house. Approximately, of course.'

A flicker of a smile crossed his face. I thought back to that time and thought of this. Where was the snag in the question? What could I say that led to danger?

I gave up. 'Five minutes or so, I would think.' And then. 'It wasn't very long because I hadn't found the light switch, which is attached to one of the beams. In the roof of the cellar.'

'Fine. Five minutes. And then what happened?'

'Well, I think it was Matty – Mathilda – my sister – she heard the sound of footsteps.'

'And where were they coming from – when you first heard them?'

I was standing on the brick floor of the cellar, smelling the damp and feeling the cold touch of fear as those feet came across the tiles from the back of the house to where we were standing. Both of us looking up. At some point Matty's hand crept into mine.

'From the kitchen. That is, from the back of the house. They came towards us.'

'And—?'

'And then stopped by the door of the cellar. We'd left it open.'

'You said in your statement to the police that the person then closed the door and locked you both in – and in fact it wasn't until your parents returned home three hours later that you were released?'

'Yes.'

'Mr Hayton,' and at this point Carlyle looked down at the sheaf of papers he was carrying, 'do you recall what the weather had been like that weekend – the weekend of the 5th and 6th of December?'

'Yes. It had snowed on the Saturday. Well, on the Friday night. I can remember because we'd gone into Craybourne shopping on the Saturday.'

'And on the Sunday, what was the ground like? Can you remember?'

That morning I'd gone out with John Franklin bike-riding. Along the path on the hill above the farm. I could remember the mud and puddles and slush.

'It was wet. There had been a bit of a thaw so there was

slush around. The ground was pretty muddy.'

' "The ground was pretty muddy",' Carlyle paused as if I'd said something of significance. And turned to the jury. 'It's worth noting, ladies and gentleman of the jury, that no trace of water or mud was found in the Hayton's house when the police arrived. And furthermore there was no evidence of forced entry to the building. The burglary becomes more and more mysterious. But that's not all, of course.

'Mr Hayton. Your father brought his work home with him?'

'Yes. He was dedicated to the – the – StarRaider project.'

'And on at least one occasion he showed you computer disks that were to be used in the aircraft?'

'Yes. Yes he did.'

'Were those disks distinctive in any way?'

Silence.

In court, in the air-conditioned cool, you couldn't even hear the sound of people in the corridor outside. Just rows of faces. Pale wood. Downlighters.

'The disks I saw, once, they had a red strip along the bottom.'

' "A red strip along the bottom".' Again that ironic repetition of what I'd said. 'Like this, for instance?' And he went over to his table, opened a document file and pulled out a black disk with the coloured marking.

'Yes.'

'And did your father leave disks like this in his study?'

'No.' I felt more confident now. Felt I was on sure ground. 'No. The only time he ever showed us the StarRaider disks, he replaced them in a special case. They were locked with some kind of security device.'

'And you never saw disks like these in his study?'

'No.'

'And when the police arrived that evening, did your father say to them that there had been a security problem? That he had left material around that was valuable or sensitive in some way?'

'No.'

'So it's unlikely that information on the StarRaider disks – computer code and so on – could have been sent on the internet that afternoon?'

I could see where he was coming from now. If the intruder hadn't sent the information then Dad was in the frame. I was helping Mr Carlyle chisel out a verdict of guilty. Because if the intruder hadn't emailed Lamplight, who had?

'Mr Hayton?'

The judge, Mr Wingate, stopped writing and looked over his desk.

'I'm sorry?'

'Without the StarRaider disks, Mr Hayton, could the information have been sent by the burglar?'

'No.' I wiped sweat from my forehead. 'No. It couldn't.'

'Thank you. No further questions.'

Twenty-nine

'What do you think Mr Bellamy?'

We were in a plain room on the ground floor of the court. A single barred window looked out on to an inner enclosure and Dad sat behind a table looking at the rotund solicitor pulling off the cellophane from a packet of cheap cigars. His opened briefcase and three coloured folders were piled on the table.

'Not a disaster, Brian, by any means. I've just—'

'Mr Bellamy, I'm not an idiot.'

In the white light cast by the neon strip, Dad's face was pale and gaunt. There was a tension about him that spread out from the screwed-up intensity of his eyes; the tightness of his mouth.

'I know it's your job to keep my spirits up—'

The solicitor raised his hand.

'Right. Listen. You haven't been found guilty of the main charge. The prosecution have presented the court with a series of facts, but these are all circumstantial. You have acknowledged that you took the disks home. It's not in doubt that the information got on to the internet – but there's nothing to prove 'beyond reasonable doubt' that *you* were responsible for emailing Lamplight.'

There was comfort in Mr Bellamy's assurance; with his friendliness and confidence. After all, I can remember thinking, he must know what he's doing.

Towards the end of the meeting, Mr Dyer, our barrister came in. He looked different out of his wig, more like a normal person I suppose rather than someone who had just flown in from the eighteenth century.

He was a tall man with receding dark hair and a prominent Adam's apple. He spoke with the voice, the accent, of someone who had grown up learning Latin and Greek at some top public school.

After he had shaken hands and said hello, he surprised us all by adding to Mr Bellamy's aura of confidence.

'Not a bad morning,' he said, smiling. 'The prosecution have a problem: they haven't a plausible theory as to why you, Brian, should have suddenly taken it into your head to give away state secrets.

'Gone bonkers? No evidence. Given large dollops of money by an enemy power? No evidence. Got a sudden conscience about working for the arms industry? The cupboard is bare.

'All they can say is that a crime has been committed but they can do no more than suggest that you are *one* of the suspects. The cross-examination of Graham was pretty desperate stuff,' and he squeezed my arm reassuringly.

* * *

When we returned to court that afternoon officials were busy putting up a screen and sorting out television link cables. The lawyers clustered in groups discussing – for all I know – their arrangements for the next weekend, whilst the reporters chatted and laughed and my immediate neighbours talked sickness and holidays.

Dad presumably reflected on his life.

And then the clerk of the court brought an abrupt silence with: 'The court will come to order' and Mr Dyer was on his feet.

'I am grateful for the court's indulgence whilst we got the technical arrangements in place. You have heard, ladies and gentleman of the jury, that the prosecution have maintained throughout that the defendant, Mr Hayton, was responsible for sending technical information about the new aircraft to a website in the United States.' He paused and looked down, as if to give the jury time to get up to speed.

'We listened this morning to the evidence of Matty's brother about what took place on the afternoon of 6th December, when the children were locked in the cellar of their house – but what of Matty herself, what was her experience on that crucial afternoon? And, more importantly, what did she notice?'

'My learned friend, Mrs Sturridge, will pick up the story with Matty.'

At which point Matty's face suddenly ballooned into the courtroom. Light flooded away behind her and, probably from some signal, she looked up from the drawing she was plainly doing and stared into the camera.

It was at this moment that I could see the point of using her as a defence witness. How could someone so young and so innocent tell anything but the truth?

'Matty?' said a voice, presumably that of Mrs Sturridge, 'I'd like to talk to you about your house.'

Matty's head was bent, her right hand scrubbing away at some paper.

'Do you remember that time when you and Graham went into the cellar?'

'When we – when the door was—?' She looked to her right. 'When we was – shut in?'

'When you were shut in.'

'It was cold. Do you wear a funny hat – like the other people?'

'Sometimes, Matty. But not now.'

'When we were in the cellar we heard the steps. They went into Daddy's room.'

She bent and scribbled away busily for a second. 'They were using Daddy's computer.'

Silence.

'How do you know that, Matty?'

'Because' – and she looked up into the camera, her eyebrows drawn in concentration – 'because I heard that funny sound the computer makes when Daddy looks up Chelsea.'

'What do you mean "that funny sound"?'

'You know – like a telephone noise.' And she giggled, and then 'it goes – kind of – beep–bip–beep–beep–beep.'

Again I was back in the cold light of last winter, listening to the silence overhead and then crossing the cellar to mount the stairs and check the door. And whilst I was gone, in those thirty seconds, Matty heard that strange slurry of high frequency sound coming from the computer. And she knew what it meant.

'Was the person using the internet, Matty?'

She didn't say anything for ten seconds and I think everyone must have thought that she hadn't heard or understood the question. But then, looking very serious, 'I think so. I thought that it was Paul–Paul Whitaker again. But I knew that Paul wouldn't–wouldn't hurt us. You know?'

There was silence.

'The person that came into the house locked the door. That person wasn't Paul.' Pause. 'Do you like my picture?'

'Matty,' said Mrs Sturridge quietly. 'Who is Paul?'

There was a long, long silence. Everyone in the court looked at the screen as though it was the last thirty seconds of a Hollywood movie.

'Paul lived in the house – years and years and years ago.' She stopped and thought for a moment. 'He was *Private* Paul Whitaker. He isn't alive any more. He tried to stop people – he tried to stop bad men making – poisonous gas.'

'So—'

'They took him away – up the hill and tied him to a chair. They said bad things about him and – covered his face. And then other men pointed their guns. And they shot him – as he sat there. That morning.'

'He's' – Matty looked into the camera again – 'he's a ghost.'

Thirty

On my desk there's an old book, a pocket watch that's stopped at eleven minutes past five and three old coins.

I can hear Matty in the garden playing with her friend Susan. They've spread a cot blanket on the grass: their dolls are having a picnic.

Mum has gone over to visit Violet Thompson in the village, although she's left the radio on in the kitchen. The to and fro of voices tells you some polite chat programme is being broadcast.

When Matty's face had been turned off, silence was switched on in the court. The judge – Mr Wingate – defence advocate, assembled lawyers and court officials, reporters and jury – the three rows of people in the visitor's gallery, were motionless – unmoving and unspeaking. Dad sat with his head in his hands.

Amidst the clutter on my desk there's a torn newspaper clipping from the *Express*, the day after Matty's evidence: *Ghost Haunts Trial* says the headline and below there's a photograph of our house, taken in December. The curtains have been closed, and there are tyre tracks in the yard. It looks deserted – and secretive.

Over everything hung the presence of Paul Whitaker. During that week, all the newspapers ran features on the plight of conscientious objectors in the First World War. The Ministry of Defence confirmed the existence of Private Whitaker, late of the Wiltshire regiment, and acknowledged that he had received a death sentence at a court martial in 1918 as a result of a serious breach of security concerning poison gas research.

The Times said they had no record of any correspondence from any Private Whitaker.

And yet whilst it became a topic for discussion in schools and offices, on radio and TV, we had to live with the continuing drama in Court Number 2 at Craybourne. When we got home that night we sat at the kitchen table drinking tea. I don't suppose any of us knew where to start and even Matty was quiet. Mum flicked through the day's paper; Matty chewed on a biscuit; I watched a spider darning its web. You could hear the bad-tempered bickering of magpies outside.

Then Mum closed the paper and spoke to us both.

'This has been a terrible, terrible ordeal. For your father, locked up and shamed; for us trying to carry on our lives as though nothing has happened.' She paused and pinched the bridge of her nose, eyes closed.

'Dad and I were proud of you both. We brought you up to tell the truth and you did just that.'

'I can't pretend to know anything about ghosts or

the supernatural, but despite the slippery tongue of the prosecution, we weren't shamed. However awkward the evidence, you didn't let us down.'

She stopped talking, bent her head and cried.

Thirty-one

Craybourne Crown Court is in the centre of town, across from the swimming baths and separated from the old woollen mill by a dual carriageway.

The court building is no more than ten years old I guess, constructed from cream-coloured stone and with a roof that splits neatly down the ridge to allow light to fall through copious sheets of glass.

I suppose when it was designed the idea was to demonstrate to the world a sense of balance and fairness about the justice system: the exact divide of the sloping roof suggesting even-handedness; the light pouring in through the windows bringing to mind honesty and truth.

You can reach the court by the subway from the swimming-pool car park and it's the place where many people attending a trial choose to leave their cars.

That Friday morning, after we'd bought a ticket for space number 163, we joined the thin traffic of swimmers, shoppers, and workers heading away from town in the direction of the seat of justice.

The strange soldier in the mist and the fierce dog that leapt out at us that first night seemed galaxies away as we sat in the gradually filling court and waited for someone to press the forward button.

Mr Bellamy came over once he'd spotted us and ran through the sequence of events due to unwind during the day and Dad looked up once before the judge appeared and produced a faded smile.

In his summing up for the jury, our advocate, Mr Dyer, was sharp and to the point about the absence of incriminating evidence that might link Dad to the transmission of an email across the Atlantic.

Furthermore, although it was accepted that 6th December was the critical day, Mr Dyer quietly pointed to the eloquent testimony of Matty – 'a small girl with sharp ears who heard the computer dialling signal that meant an email was being sent on a wintery afternoon when her father was far from home.'

And as for bringing classified computer disks home, Mr Hayton had *offered* this fact to the police, and what could be construed from this other than the behaviour of a man dedicated to his work and proud of his role in the development of the technology?

Yet, unseen and unsaid, it was the ghost of Paul Whitaker that brooded over the speech. You could feel that everyone was waiting for some mention, some reference to the hand of the dead man. That other defendant in that other trial.

It was to be the prosecution who seized this weapon and turned it against us.

Standing tall in his black gown and grey wig, Mr Roger Carlyle QC rubbed the side of his expensive red nose and spoke to the jury, touching on the main points of the case, the statements made by the various witnesses, the claims put forward by the defence, and then: 'This is a perplexing case in many ways. The defence have made great play of the fact that there doesn't appear to be a motive for Brian Hayton's behaviour.

'And yet the facts *are* clear. The defendant was working on a top secret project, which involved state-of-the-art computer programming. Strictly against the policy of the company and also against the law of the land' – pause – 'he took the programming disks home on numerous occasions and even *boasted* about the project and his role in it to his family.

'This information, about which only he had access, was published on a website and the defendant's address included as a point of contact.

'We don't know what motivated Brian Hayton. We don't believe in travellers breaking into the house, neighbours with a grudge – or most improbably, Matty's ghost. That an unfortunate soldier did exist and was imprisoned in Sentinel House many years ago is an interesting fact of history. It is also an interesting fact of law that both Paul Whitaker and Brian Hayton were charged with substantially the same crime.

'Then, as now, betraying the interests of this country has been regarded as a highly serious offence. We no longer execute those found guilty of treason, but we do expect them to pay a heavy price for their shameful activities.

'The facts *are* clear and I would argue, members of the jury, that you have no alternative but to find the defendant guilty as charged.'

When the jury was sent out to consider their verdict, we were free to take lunch, wander the corridors of the court, seek silent comfort from each other. It was as though Dad had died and that we were left with memories of the man who had once walked through our lives. The Dad who told stories of Brunel, who was hooked on technology, who was consumed by the company who employed him.

And all the time, a sickness that I might have helped slam a cell door.

That day, as we gathered in the open area on the first floor, the smell of cigar smoke enveloping us, Mr Bellamy just patted my arm: 'Never second-guess a jury, son,' he said.

And it was at this time, as we sat miserably on a bench watching the eddies of lawyers and secretaries and journalists, that Matty touched my forearm with her hand, and briefly turned off the ache and the anguish as we waited for the verdict.

At that moment, the normal chatter of words going through my head, the verbal traffic that passes for thought, was filled with a different voice that was not my own.

It was quiet and at first seemed to be coming from a distance – like from the end of a long corridor – but when I concentrated, when I really tuned in, I could hear a young man speaking with a quiet clear Wiltshire accent. The voice said:

'Come ye blessed of my Father, inherit the kingdom prepared for you from the foundation of the world;

For I was an hungred, and ye gave me meat; I was thirsty and ye gave me drink: I was a stranger, and ye took me in;

Naked, and ye clothed me: I was sick, and ye visited me: I was in prison and ye came unto me.'

The jury re-entered the court at 2.40 that afternoon.

We sat in the first row in the visitors' area, directly opposite the packed seats of the press gallery. To our right, Dad behind glass; before him, rows of black gowns and wigs, and then, diagonally opposite, the jury filing awkwardly into court. The eighteen-year-old man; the grey-haired woman, the sharply dressed car salesman – and those others who had weighed the evidence for three hours.

'Have you reached a verdict upon which you are all agreed?' asked the clerk, a woman with long hair tied back in a pony-tail.

'Yes,' said the foreman of the jury, pushing the bridge of his glasses.

'Do you find the defendant guilty on the first count, that

without lawful authority he disclosed information which had been in his possession, contrary to Section 2 of the 1989 Official Secrets Act?'

The foreman coughed into his hand.

'Not guilty,' he said.

Thirty-two

The side door slams below and the criss-cross chat on the radio ceases: Mum has returned from the village.

'I'm back, Graham. Has everything been all right with Matty and Susan?'

'Fine,' I call. 'And no phone calls either.'

You can hear the two children below filling up the paddling-pool in order to bathe their dolls. It's early June and for two days temperatures have been in the lower twenties. Yesterday the field beyond the wall was filled with the noise of cows as our local farmer pushed them into new pasture. Today it threatens rain – great clods of cumulus begin to form over Wilson's Wood.

And yet the house is calm. Maybe because night doesn't press against the windows and the events of last winter are finally over; maybe because somewhere a young man who felt he'd failed in his own life had seen the demons driven away in ours and no longer walks the dark.

Despite that, I know this is the hard part, the end of the story that didn't turn out all right. Not for everybody, because after the excitement of the not-guilty verdict, and the sudden babble of whispered conversation, with reporters quietly leaving the court to phone their news rooms, the judge discharged the jury and then listened as our advocate, Mr Dyer, explained to his honour why he should look leniently on the defendant when considering a sentence for the lesser charge of taking the computer disks home.

And at length, as the court again drew in its breath, and as Dad stood looking at his honour across the heads of the barristers and solicitors, the judge, Mr Wingate, said: 'Brian Hayton, you have pleaded guilty to failing to take proper care of highly classified information, the result of which is the release to the world of computer codes which lie at the heart of a revolutionary new fighter plane.

'I have listened to testimonials from a variety of people working in the industry who make it clear that you are a clever man who has made a major contribution to British technological development. You are undoubtedly gifted and hard-working and possess the kind of skills that this country clearly has great need to cultivate.

'However, you have also displayed crass stupidity in failing to safeguard the material upon which you had been working and with which you had been entrusted. Years of work and the toil of many others has been wasted because you did not ensure the security of the data in your care. Your enthusiasm for the work and your dedication to the project are not in question and nor is your loyalty to Britain. However, you knowingly broke Section 8 of the 1989

Official Secrets Act and you are hereby sentenced to nine months' imprisonment.'

This year a pair of swallows has built a nest just above where I sit. They feed their young in rotation, winging backwards and forwards as the sky changes colour and shadows fall across the garden. Mum has planted some herbs underneath the kitchen window and we have seen hedgehogs most evenings. Over by the wall, where Matty found the badge, there's a clump of stinging nettles and some poppies.

Tomorrow is Tuesday and we're going to have breakfast early and get into the car and drive to Borough Bridge. And at 11 o'clock the small door of the prison will open, a middle-aged man with wavy hair will emerge – and we'll be together again.

Postscript

The reader has now in their possession a more complete version of the facts surrounding the trial of Brian Hayton than might have been found from newspaper reports alone.

The family has since recovered from its ordeal and was anxious to cooperate in the writing of this account. Although Mr Hayton obviously didn't return to his post at Spere Electronics, he obtained work as a freelance designer of business software.

Matty's distress during the trial of her father gradually eased with his return to the family home and with her acceptance that he wouldn't suddenly be whisked away again.

No one has subsequently been charged with the crime, although the police have kept the file open in the hope of securing a future conviction. It would certainly be libellous to indicate, as a result of my own researches, where I feel the burden of guilt might lie – but the reader is now holding the evidence and is free to speculate.

No one has ever been able to explain satisfactorily Matty's knowledge of Paul Whitaker and although sceptics have suggested that she got wind of her brother's research into the circumstances surrounding Whitaker's life and death – and that is what came out during the trial – that doesn't explain the other episodes Graham's story highlights, nor does it explain the damage to the Hayton home that occurred during the night of 10th December – the very evening when American defence consultants visited Sentinel House.

Could it have been the work of passing vandals who simply decided to give vent to violent feelings on a convenient house? Or, more spectacularly, was this the work of other forces from another time, perhaps that silent army of men, shot at dawn throughout the First World War, whose absent names haunt war memorials across Britain?

Acknowledgements

The extract on page *v* from *The Dhammapada*, translated by Juan Mascaró, 1973, Harmondsworth, London, (page 35, lines 1–6) is reproduced by permission of Penguin Books Ltd.

Another Hodder Children's book

BLOOM OF YOUTH

Moving Times One

Rachel Anderson

How was I to know that this rambling country Paradise couldn't last? They say we're in the bloom of youth. Ripe for transformation from uncouth savages to marriageable young ladies. But my sister says that out there is REAL LIFE. Bursting with passion. Love. Fulfilment. We've got to find it.

For young Ruth the future beckons, rich with dreams. But this is the 1950s. There's no halfway between girlhood and womanhood. So where does a schoolgirl seek Life and Hope? Before it slips away, beyond reach?

Another Hodder Children's book

GRANDMOTHER'S FOOTSTEPS

Moving Times Two

Rachel Anderson

I do so much want to follow in her footsteps. On the day the war ended, Granny told me to stick by her and I'd be all right. I'm trying to do just that, to stay as close to her as I can, for ever and ever.

But Ruth's mother, returning from the Victory celebrations, has quite other plans for the family's future. So, in the unfamiliar post-war world, begins a succession of wild schemes, changes and upheavals, different homes, new babies, encounters with strangers. And devastating loss and sadness. But ever present, for young Ruth, is the certain echo of her Granny's footsteps.